"You Still Deal With Everything You Find Difficult By Refusing To Talk About It,"

Kristin said. "Don't look now, Secret Agent Man, but that's a coward's way out." She watched as a muscle tightened in his whisker-bristled cheek.

"What did you expect, Kristin? A few stanzas of poetry? A declaration of my undying love?"

The words wounded Kristin far more cruelly than she would ever have guessed they could. "No, Zachary," she answered, with a calmness that surprised her. "Not from you." Her ire simmered and bubbled, but she wouldn't let him see. "I wouldn't have let you make love to me," she said stiffly, "if I hadn't been so scared. It won't happen again."

Zachary tossed her a cocky grin underlaid with cold steel. "We've got a long way to go before we're out of Cabriz, princess," he replied. "So don't be too sure of yourself."

Dear Reader:

Welcome to the world of Silhouette Desire. Join me as we travel to a land of incredible passion and tantalizing romance—a place where dreams can, and do, come true.

When I read a Silhouette Desire, I sometimes feel as if I'm going on a little vacation. I can relax, put my feet up and become transported to a new world...a world that has, naturally, a perfect hero just waiting to whisk me away! These are stories to remember, containing moments to treasure.

Silhouette Desire novels are romantic love stories— sensuous yet emotional. As a reader, you not only see the hero and heroine fall in love, you also feel what they're feeling.

In upcoming books look for some of your favorite Silhouette Desire authors: Joan Hohl, BJ James, Linda Lael Miller and Diana Palmer.

So enjoy!

Lucia Macro
Senior Editor

LINDA
LAEL MILLER
ESCAPE FROM CABRIZ

SILHOUETTE *Desire*

Published by Silhouette Books New York

America's Publisher of Contemporary Romance

Books by Linda Lael Miller

Silhouette Intimate Moments

Snowflakes on the Sea #59
Part of the Bargain #87

Silhouette Special Edition

State Secrets #277
Ragged Rainbows #324

Silhouette Desire

Used-to-Be Lovers #438
Only Forever #480
Just Kate #516
Daring Moves #547
Mixed Messages #568
Escape from Cabriz #589

LINDA LAEL MILLER

delights in creating passionate, believable characters and dramatic plots. She loves to travel to research her books, and dreams of visiting faraway places with strange-sounding names. She lives in Port Orchard, Washington, with her daughter, Wendy.

For Cheryl, Chris, and April,
dear and special friends.

One

The roar of the ocean followed Zachary Harmon across the weathered deck and inside his beach house. Shivering with cold, he pushed the sliding glass door closed and peeled off his sodden blue sweatshirt, tossing it into the oversize closet where the washer and drier were hidden. Then he hooked his thumbs under the waistband of his orange running shorts.

He was just about to remove them and send them flying after the sweatshirt when the flickering screen of the small color TV affixed to the underside of one of the kitchen cupboards drew his attention. As usual, he'd forgotten to turn it off before going out.

The pit of Zachary's stomach did a carnival-ride pitch-and-spin as he stood there in the middle of the kitchen floor, dripping rainwater and staring.

The voice of the TV anchorman seemed to weave in and out of his consciousness. "The political climate in the small Southeast Asian country of Cabriz is worsening by the hour as warring factions grapple for control of the government. A spokesman for the State Department says Americans in Cabriz may be in serious danger...embassies being closed..."

Zachary shut his eyes momentarily against an onslaught of memories and fears. The Cabrizian man-on-the-street was a pretty laid-back guy, mostly concerned with harvesting a few acres of rice and keeping his ox from being repossessed, but some of the rebels were into imaginative atrocities.

And Kristin was in Cabriz.

The newscaster went on to another subject, after promising regular updates on the situation in Southeast Asia, and Zachary snapped off the TV set. He stood with his hands braced against the counter, mentally sifting through all the memorized data he had on Cabriz—which was considerable, since he'd spent so much time there while he'd been with the agency.

He went to the other counter and poured a cup of coffee. There were several rebel factions in Cabriz—all made up of wild-eyed fanatics bent on overthrowing the existing dictatorship. Just twenty-four hours before, the beleaguered government had broken off diplomatic relations with the United States, Great Britain and Canada because of their refusal to step in militarily.

Kristin, by an act of supreme idiocy, had aligned herself with the royal family. Zachary raised the mug of steaming coffee to his mouth and cursed when he burned his tongue. The fact that Kristin planned to marry Jascha, the crown prince of Cabriz, was still difficult to accept.

It wounded him that their time together had meant so little to her.

Zachary set the mug down with a thump. Kristin's position was precarious, to say the least; she would be roughly as popular in Cabriz as Marie Antoinette had been in Paris after the fall of the Bastille.

The fingers of Zachary's right hand knotted into a fist, and he pounded the counter once, to vent some of his frustration. Kristin couldn't really be in love with that guy; it wasn't possible.

Because he needed something to do, he reached for the telephone receiver and punched out a number he'd never forgotten.

"Perry King's office," a pleasant female voice chimed.

"This is Zachary Harmon," was the brusque reply. "Put me through."

The secretary hesitated for only a moment, then there was a blipping sound and Perry came on the line.

"Hello, Zachary," he said warmly.

Zachary stated his business, sparing the polite preamble. "What idiot let Kristin Meyers leave for Cabriz when the damn government is collapsing?"

Perry sighed heavily. "She went there to marry the crown prince. Besides, she's the daughter of an ambassador turned cabinet member, in case you've forgotten. It probably took one phone call."

"Any plans to go in after her?"

"God knows, the Secretary wants her out of there yesterday, but we can't forget that Miss Meyers is in the country of her own free will. After all, she's—er—well, like I said, she's supposed to be getting married any day now."

A shaft of pain speared Zachary's middle. "Dammit, P.K., that airhead socialite probably doesn't have the first idea of what she's messing with. Chances are, the prince is planning to use her as leverage to get the administration to step in with military aid. And you know their position on that!"

"Zach, are you volunteering to go in?"

Zachary thought of the quiet, peaceful life he'd built for himself. No demands, no pressures, no emergency missions in the middle of the night. He didn't even have a dog to feed.

He had things set up just the way he wanted them. He taught political science at Silver Shores Junior College, because it was easy and because it allowed him to live near the ocean, and he grew tomatoes in clay pots.

"Zachary?" his friend and former employer prompted.

"Yes, dammit," Zachary replied, thinking of defiant green eyes and long brown hair that caught the sunlight and turned it to fire. "I want to go in and get Kristin. And don't remind me that I resigned from the agency eighteen months ago. Nobody's better qualified, even now."

Perry sighed again. "That's true. But I can't just give you the go-ahead—I have to make a few calls before I can do that. So sit tight—you hear me?"

"I hear you," Zachary grumbled, then hung up with a crash. He was already planning to leave within the next twenty-four hours, whether the trip was sanctioned by Washington or not. He knew a thousand ways in and out of Cabriz.

An hour later, showered and clad in blue jeans, dry sneakers and a navy sweatshirt, Zachary stood at the stove, stirring a pan of canned spaghetti and watching another update on the cable news channel. The telephone jangled, and he had the receiver in his hand before the first ring faded.

"Harmon," he snapped.

The answering voice belonged to one of the president's favorite men—and Zachary's *least* favorite—Kristin's father. "This is Kenyan Meyers. I've just spent some time on the telephone with Perry King, over at the State Department. He tells me you're willing to go into Cabriz and bring Kristin home."

"That's right," Zachary replied. He wasn't awed by Meyers; he'd dealt with more powerful men, but he was on guard because of all that had happened between him and Kristin. And because he knew the Secretary was about as benevolent as a cobra with PMS.

Meyers paused for a moment before replying. "You're aware, of course, that Kristin may well want to stay in Cabriz. Especially if the marriage has already taken place."

"I'll take that chance."

"Fine. One of our planes will pick you up in Seattle in exactly ten hours—you know the procedure, I'm sure. You'll be briefed on the current state of affairs during the flight."

"Thanks." Zachary was moving to hang up when Meyers spoke again. He put the receiver back to his ear.

"Bring my daughter home, Harmon, whether she's agreeable or not. She has no idea what kind of situation she's gotten herself into."

The only thing Zachary could have promised anyone at that point was that if Kristin was still alive when he arrived in Cabriz, he was going to strangle her personally. And he wasn't laboring under any flowery delusions that Meyers's true concerns were for Kristin. He definitely had some important political ax to grind. "I'll be in contact with you as soon as I can, Mr. Secretary," Zachary replied evenly, and the call was over.

Kristin's bravado was beginning to desert her as she stood beside a veiled servant woman at one of the windows, watching as Jascha's troops drilled in the dusty streets of the city of Kiri, Cabriz's capital. The place seemed so different now, so unfamiliar. It was hard to believe she'd grown up only a few blocks away, in the American embassy.

With a sigh, Kristin sank into a rattan chair, one blue-jeaned leg slung over the arm, and let her head fall back. She closed her eyes and thought of the day she'd left Cabriz, at seventeen. She'd finished her high school work, with the help of her tutor, and now it was time to return to America....

"I don't want to leave you," she sniffled, looking up at Jascha's face though a blur of tears. Overhead a lemon tree blossomed, dropping delicate white petals all around them, like snow.

Jascha was a prince, in every sense of the word. With his dark hair and eyes and exquisitely tailored clothes, he could have stepped out of the pages of a storybook. He kissed her lightly on the forehead, his strong hands holding her shoulders. "Do not cry, Kristin," he said, his voice a ragged whisper. "One day you will come back to Cabriz, and you and I will reign together."

Kristin swallowed, hardly daring to believe the fairy tale even though she and Jascha had discussed it many times. "But your father has seven wives," she said, echoing her mother's pet reason why nothing could ever come of Jascha and Kristin's bittersweet romance.

Jascha traced the line of her cheek with a smooth thumb. "You will be my only wife, little lemon flower. This I promise you."

Kristin believed him, perhaps because she was seventeen and he was the first man she'd ever loved, and threw herself into his arms even as her father called impatiently from the other side of the embassy courtyard. Jascha kissed her soundly before stepping aside, his hands caught together behind his back, to await the ambassador's appearance.

Almost regretfully, Kristin came back to the here and now. Her parents had looked upon her earlier relationship with Jascha as a teenage infatuation and therefore hadn't taken it too seriously, but they were strenuously opposed to the marriage that was about to take place. Even if the political system hadn't been in chaos, they probably wouldn't have attended the wedding.

Kristin sighed, possessed by a strange loneliness. She loved Jascha, she insisted to herself. She had loved him since childhood, when the two of them had played on the palace lawn.

But it wasn't Jascha's handsome face that came into her thoughts as she rose from her chair and went to stand looking out on the courtyard. It was Zachary Harmon's.

Just the memory made her furious. She had no business thinking about Zachary—he was nothing but a self-centered adventurer, afraid of commitment and responsibility. She'd never really cared for him.

The swift, secret sensations in Kristin's body gave the lie to that idea. Maybe the emotional attachment had ended, but she still felt a physical response every time he invaded her mind.

Mercifully, she reflected with a lift of her chin, that didn't happen often.

She turned from the glass door and surveyed the sumptuous bedroom that would be hers until after the wedding ceremony. There was a lovely gauzy white spread on the enormous teakwood bed, and rattan chairs with bright floral cushions were everywhere. In less than twenty-four hours Kristin would leave this room for Jascha's.

She sank her teeth into her lower lip as she went to a nearby table and picked up her camera. She wondered what kind of lover Jascha would be, then put the thought out of her mind. She would find that out soon enough.

After attaching the telephoto lens, Kristin carried her camera back to the terrace door, focused and began taking pictures of Jascha's troops drilling in the courtyard. "The photo-diary of a future princess," she muttered to herself.

Kristin was so involved in picture taking that she didn't hear the door of her room open, didn't know Jascha was there until he turned her gently to face him.

As always, she was struck by his imperial good looks. His exiled father was Asian, but his mother had come from India, and he had her round, dark eyes. He wore slacks, a jacket and a tailored shirt, putting on his uniform only for state occasions. He took the camera from her hands—a little impatiently, it seemed to Kristin—and set it aside.

"Do you wish to go back to the United States?" he asked, glancing over her shoulder at the troops she'd been capturing on film. "There could be war at any moment."

Kristin had some feelings she didn't want to explore just then, but she'd been well trained in the art of loyalty. She smiled, laid her hands on Jascha's broad shoulders and shook her head. The two of them had played together as children, fallen in love as teenagers, and later Jascha had persuaded his father to allow him to go to college in Massachusetts—the same one Kristin had attended. They'd dated steadily then.

Later, when Kristin had moved to California to work on an advanced degree and Jascha had returned home, they had written each other long, soul-searching letters.

Until Zachary came along, that is. Kristin had truly thought she was in love with him—it must have been the secret-agent mystique—and even moved into his apartment.

Kristin had crawled away from that relationship, emotionally speaking, not caring whether she lived or died. It had been Jascha who had made the difference; somehow he'd learned what had happened and he'd come to her. Twenty-four hours a day he'd pursued her, sending flowers and jewelry, whisking her off to other parts of the world in his private jet, promising he would never, ever hurt her.

In her vulnerable position, it had been easy to buy into the fantasy. Now, far from her friends and family, Kristin was beginning to come out of the daze induced by her breakup with Zachary, and she could no longer ignore her doubts.

Jascha bent his head and kissed her, lightly at first and then with increasing passion. Kristin waited to feel some kind of physical response, as she had in the old days, before Zachary, but nothing happened.

Still unwilling to face the growing suspicion that she'd made a disastrous mistake, Kristin marked her coolness down to prewedding jitters.

There was a certain sadness in Jascha's dark eyes as he drew back to look at her. The edge of his thumb grazed her cheek lightly as he muttered, "Kristin. My lovely, lovely Kristin. I am afraid for you. I should not have brought you here."

In the distance Kristin heard the ominous popping sound of gunshots, and the drilling of the troops went on. She forced herself to smile. "Whatever happens, Jascha, I want to be with you."

He bent to nibble at the side of her neck, and one of his hands lightly cupped her breast.

To her own surprise, as much as Jascha's, Kristin bolted backward out of his embrace.

Jascha was not without temperament, and his well-sculpted lips formed a royal pout. "You still think of him," he accused. "The man you lived with in California."

Kristin shook her head, acutely aware that he was right. "No. it's just that—it's just that I think we should wait. Until after our wedding."

He folded his strong arms and cocked his head to one side, and for the first time, Kristin knew he was consider-

ing forcing her. Although he had always been kind, she was
well aware of Jascha's legendary temper.

"You want to keep yourself chaste," he said evenly. "Yet
for twelve months you slept in Zachary Harmon's bed.
Surely you see that we have a contradiction in terms here."

Kristin retreated another step. Jascha had never used this
tone with her before; it had to be the stresses of his precarious political situation. "The time I spent with Zachary was
a mistake," she answered evenly. "If I could go back and
change it, I would."

Jascha advanced toward her, trapping her between himself and the bed. "You will find me a more than satisfactory lover," he said in a low voice, pulling the tails of her
cotton shirt from her jeans.

Panic wrapped itself around Kristin like a lash, sudden
and strange. Where once she had burned to give herself to
this man, now she was frightened, even repulsed, by his
touch. "Jascha, no," she whispered, crossing her forearms
in front of her chest and struggling to stay upright.

He flung her onto the bed and held her wrists together
high above her head. With his free hand, he began unbut-
toning her shirt.

Kristin twisted, trying vainly to break away, filled with
fear and rage. The warnings she'd heard from her parents
and friends screamed in her mind. *He'll have absolute control over you—in his culture, women are property—you've
only seen the Jascha he wanted you to see....*

Just as Jascha bared one of Kristin's breasts and closed
his hand over it, the door of the bedroom opened and Mai
entered, carrying tea. Although her eyes were downcast, as
became a lowly servant in the presence of her prince, she
obviously knew what was going on. And she wasn't about
to leave.

Jascha muttered a curse and released Kristin, storming out of the room and slamming the door behind him.

Too mortified to meet Mai's gaze, Kristin sat up, righted her bra and buttoned her shirt. Because she didn't know what to say, she was silent.

Mai busied herself laying out the tiny bowls in which tea was served, along with the small sweet cakes she knew Kristin loved. "Weather is hot. Perhaps Miss Kristin like to bathe in swimming pool," she said, pretending nothing out of the ordinary had happened.

Kristin felt sick. Something was wrong with Jascha—terribly wrong. In all the years she'd known him, he'd never mistreated her in any way, though she had to admit he'd been damnably arrogant on occasion. Yet only moments before, he'd been bent on raping her. Ignoring the tea, she made for the telephone at her bedside.

"I'm in no mood to swim," she muttered, while silently cursing herself for every kind of romantic fool. She should have seen this coming. She should have known she'd only been trying to revive her old feelings for Jascha because she couldn't bear the pain of grieving for Zachary. "I want to call my father."

"Line's cut," Mai said succinctly.

Kristin felt the color drain out of her face as she lifted the ornate receiver and put it to her ear. Sure enough, there was no dial tone, only an ominous silence.

But Jascha had offered to send her home to the United States before he'd gotten so angry and thrown her onto the bed. She had to find him, tell him she'd changed her mind.

She strode to the door and wrenched it open, her rising ire lending her courage as she marched along the elegantly carpeted hallway, down the curving stairs that led to the great entryway with its glittering crystal chandeliers.

A guard was posted by the front door. "Where is the prince?" she demanded, heedless of her untucked shirt and mussed hair.

The guard's expression didn't change. "There," he said in Cabrizian, pointing toward the towering double doors of Jascha's study with the barrel of his rifle.

Kristin knocked briskly, then marched inside without waiting for an invitation. Jascha was in hushed conference with one of his generals, and his glowering expression said he did not appreciate the interruption.

"I've changed my mind about everything," Kristin announced. "The wedding is off. I want to go home right now."

For a moment she saw the old tenderness in Jascha's eyes, but then they turned hard as ebony. "It is too late," he bit out, while the general looked on unabashedly. "Go to your room, Kristin, and do not come out again until you are told."

Kristin's mouth fell open, and she stood rooted to the center of the study floor. She was twenty-seven years old, and she hadn't been sent to her room in two decades. She wasn't about to set a new precedent.

"Go!" Jascha said with a dismissive wave of one hand.

Instead, Kristin stepped closer to him. "What's happened to you?" she whispered. "Why are you behaving like this?"

"This is Cabriz, not America," Jascha pointed out. "Things are different here. Now, do as I say before I decide you must be disciplined."

"Disciplined?" Kristin's fury was so great that it rose into her throat and swelled, making it impossible for any more words to pass.

Jascha was livid. He called out a word Kristin couldn't translate, and the guard from the entryway appeared. A rapid conversation passed between them, of which Kristin caught only a few words. Then the guard took her arm and dragged her roughly toward the door.

Kristin struggled, but it was no use. "Jascha!" she cried, in an angry plea for reason, as she was propelled out of the study and up the stairs.

Minutes later, Kristin was flung unceremoniously into a large room and the door was locked behind her.

Wildly, she looked around. The place was huge, and sumptuously furnished. The chairs and sofas were all upholstered in colorful silk, and heavy damask curtains surrounded the enormous bed, which stood on a dais. There was an ivory fireplace, even though the temperature in that part of Cabriz never dipped low enough for a fire, and a beautiful Louis XIV desk stood in front of the windows.

Kristin's anger reached ferocious proportions when she realized that this was Jascha's room, and she'd been sent here, like a mischievous concubine, to await the prince's convenience. She hurled herself at the giant door, hammering at it with both fists and screaming, "Let me out! Damn you, Jascha, *let me out*!"

After a while Kristin sagged against the wood, exhausted. It was hopeless; no one in the palace, not even Mai, would dare to flout Jascha's authority by releasing her. She was going to have to find her own means of escape.

She went to the terrace doors. For a moment Kristin had hope, but then she looked over the stone railing. It was at least a thirty-foot drop to the courtyard below, and there were no trees or trellises to climb down.

Momentarily defeated, she went back inside, out of the blazing midafternoon sun.

She searched the desk drawers for a key, but found nothing other than a stack of letters scented with some spicy perfume and written in Cabrizian. Although Kristin could understand the language if it was spoken slowly and clearly, she had never learned to read it.

Still, it didn't take a genius to figure out that the letters had been written by a woman. Feeling more a fool than ever, Kristin put the envelopes back where she'd found them and continued her exploration.

After an hour, when she'd found nothing that would aid in her escape and had exhausted herself emotionally, she collapsed in the middle of Jascha's enormous bed. She awakened sometime later to find herself surrounded by women, all veiled, all clad in the colorful, gauzy robes worn by Cabrizian females.

Mai was not among them.

"What the hell?" Kristin gasped, bolting upright and trying to scramble off the bed, but the women wouldn't let her pass. They gripped her arms and legs, and one of them clasped the back of her neck in strong fingers. She struggled, but there were too many of them, and they subdued her. "Who are you?" she cried. "What do you want?"

"Open mouth," one of them ordered. Gone were the gentle, subservient tones that had always been used with her before.

"Let go of me!" Kristin ordered. "Right now!"

When the women ignored her, she threw her head back and screamed Jascha's name.

Her right arm was wrenched behind her back and pulled painfully upward. The command was repeated.

Kristin had no choice but to obey. She parted her lips, and a bitter-tasting wine was poured onto her tongue. Not daring to spit it out, she swallowed convulsively. "Stupid," she muttered, addressing herself, coming face-to-face with a reality she'd refused to consider before. *"Stupid!"*

The women were stripping her clothes away, but when Kristin moved to fight them again, she found that her muscles had turned to rice pudding. She was helpless.

Her eyes filled with tears of frustration and fear. Jascha had lied, both to her and her family. These women were his wives.

She was raised from the bed and propelled into the prince's private bath, where an enormous tub of inlaid tiles waited, filled with steaming, scented water.

The women—she tried counting them, but could not think clearly—lowered her into the tub and, remarkably, began to bathe her. They surrounded her and their swift, firm hands were everywhere, soaping her arms and legs, lathering her hair.

After a while Kristin was lulled into a state of half consciousness. They lifted her from the tub and dried her as carefully as they'd bathed her, and then she was ushered back to the bed again.

She felt silken sheets against her bare back as they laid her down. Now, she thought dreamily, they would let her rest.

But they didn't. They began rubbing scented oil into her skin, covering her breasts, her stomach, her thighs. Something stirred in Kristin; she felt herself drifting through space, back to another time and another place.

"Zachary," she whispered with a soft smile.

Her skin was powdered, her hair dried and brushed. Kristin lost track of time and reality.

A familiar masculine voice disturbed her erotic dreams. "Okay, princess, wake up. We're going home."

Slowly, Kristin opened her eyes. For a moment she thought she was still sleeping, because Zachary's shadowed face was looming in the darkness, only inches from hers. "Zachary?"

"That's me," he replied, reaching under her and lifting her off the mattress. "It's a good thing they used powder after they greased you," he said, holding her up with one arm and pulling rough cotton trousers onto her with the other. "Otherwise you'd be slippery as hell and I'd probably drop you right on your hard little head. Not that it would make any real difference in your thinking processes...."

The effects of the drug the wives had forced on Kristin were just beginning to wear off, but she still felt woozy and very unsteady on her feet. She shook her head. "Zachary, is that really you?"

"It's really me, princess. And keep your voice down. If His Highness finds me in the royal boudoir, I'll be in for a rough three or four days in the dungeon."

He pulled a shirt over her head and forced her arms into the sleeves. Then she rested her cheek against his chest, yawning. "How did you find me?"

"That's a long story. We'll talk about it when we're at least fifty miles from this place." He caught a curved finger under her chin. "Maybe it's a good thing you're stoned out of your mind," he confided. "We're about to climb down over the terrace, and there's always a possibility one of the guards might wake up. Whatever you do, princess, hold on tight and keep that legendary mouth shut."

Before Kristin could lodge any kind of protest, Zachary hoisted her over one shoulder and headed toward the terrace doors. It was dark and the ebony sky was littered with stars. When she saw the stone railing approaching, Kristin squeezed her eyes shut and sucked in a breath.

"Now remember," Zachary told her in a rough undertone, *"be quiet."*

There was an awful jostling sensation, and Kristin caught hold of the back of Zachary's belt and hung on with all her strength. The fact that she'd been drugged did nothing to ease her fear when she opened her eyes and saw that they were descending a thin rope into the dark courtyard.

If she hadn't still been holding her breath, she would have screamed her lungs out.

Presently they reached the ground and Zachary set Kristin on her feet, where she teetered for a moment, to flip the grappling hook loose from the terrace railing and wind the rope around one hand. Kristin lifted her hand to her mouth to stifle another yawn. "You'll never believe what just happened to me in there—"

Even in the thin light of an autumn moon, Kristin saw the muscle tighten in his jaw. "I've got a pretty good idea," he responded. "Now, let's get out of here."

Once they'd gained the palace wall, Zachary flung the grappling hook over the top, then wrenched on the rope to make sure it was secure.

"Not again," Kristin protested.

"Get on my back," Zachary ordered impatiently. "And for God's sake, stop bitching. In case you haven't noticed, your ladyship, I'm doing all the damn work!"

Kristin put her arms around his neck and climbed onto him piggyback style. "Think of it as just recompense for all the times I had to carry out the garbage and wash your socks," she replied sweetly, her head clearing by the moment.

He started up the wall. "You never had to wash my socks," he retorted, his voice sounding choked.

Kristin loosened her grip slightly. "It was a metaphor," she whispered back.

"You know," he grunted in response, straining to pull them both up the rope, "the prince probably deserves you. Maybe I should take you back there and let them finish the ritual."

They'd reached the top of the wall, and Kristin could just rely make out the outline of a Jeep below.

"Jump," Zachary instructed her. "We're like ducks in a shooting gallery up here."

Kristin's heart hammered in her chest. "I'm not jumping!" she protested. "It must be ten feet to the ground!"

"Aim for the bushes," Zachary answered, and then his hand pressed into the small of her back and she went sailing off the wall. He landed in the shrubbery only a moment after she did.

She flew at him, hands flying, bones aching from a jarring touchdown.

He caught her wrists and stayed the attack, and his perfect teeth flashed in an acid grin as he looked down at her. "No time for gratitude, princess. It won't be long before they miss you."

Kristin started to say that she didn't want to go anywhere with him, but the memory of Jascha hurling her onto the bed stopped her. If Mai hadn't come in when she had, Prince Charming would have slapped her senseless and then raped her. Anything was better than a lifetime of that. "If we hurry," she said with a meekness she didn't feel, "we can get to the Canadian embassy before Jascha's servants sound the alarm. It's just around the corner."

Zachary thrust her into the jeep and got behind the wheel. "There isn't any Canadian embassy," he answered as they drove quickly away from the palace wall. "Not anymore. Hold on to your pedigree, princess—we're leaving Cabriz the hard way."

Two

Zachary wheeled the Jeep through dark, narrow streets Kristin didn't recognize. The city seemed strangely quiet. Empty.

"Where is everybody?" Kristin asked, raising her voice to be heard.

"Hiding. This is a military Jeep."

Kristin swallowed and brushed her tangled hair back from her face with both hands. "You mean, people think we're soldiers?"

"Probably."

Uneasily, Kristin ran her hands down her thighs. She was wearing the pajamalike garb of Cabrizian peasantry, male or female. "Where did you get it?"

"I stole it," he answered with exaggerated politeness. "Given your station in life, I tried to get an embassy limo with little flags on the hood, but they were all booked up—it must be prom night."

Kristin's temper rose steadily as they left the ancient city behind and started up a nearby mountain. As far as she could tell, there wasn't any road. She folded her arms across her breasts. "Still jealous of the advantages I've had," she replied. "Honestly, Zachary, envy doesn't become you."

The Jeep stopped with a jolt. "Let's get one thing straight, princess. Anybody who wanted your life—" he jabbed at his temple with an angry forefinger "—would have to be one can short of a six-pack. And if you wouldn't mind, how about a little gratitude? I didn't have to take this job, you know!"

Kristin subsided, stung. She hadn't had a chance to prepare for this encounter with Zachary, and the pain was intense. "You didn't even ask if I wanted to leave," she observed in a more moderate tone of voice.

Zachary guided the intrepid little vehicle into even more inhospitable terrain. There were towering pine trees all around, and enormous boulders. "Well, excuse me," he replied dramatically. "I'll drop you off at the next corner!"

"Stop yelling," Kristin said with a sigh. Zachary hadn't changed in the year and a half since she'd seen him. He was still bristly and uncommunicative—the dedicated agent through and through. "We're going to be together for a few hours, so we might as well try to get along."

The Jeep came to another lurching stop, and Zachary turned to her, smiling in amazed amusement. "A few hours?"

"Sure. There's a helicopter hidden around here somewhere, isn't there?"

He gave a hoot of derisive laughter.

"What's funny?" Kristin demanded.

"You are. There isn't any helicopter, your ladyship. We're going to travel through the mountains on horseback. If we're lucky—*damn* lucky—we'll be over the border into Rhaos in five days.''

Kristin gulped. For a moment she actually considered turning back, going through with the marriage to Jascha. Held up alongside the prospect of five days with Zachary Harmon, under the harshest of conditions, life in the palace didn't look so bad. "Oh," she said.

Zachary jammed the jeep into gear, and they were moving up the mountain again. When they'd traveled for what seemed like hours to Kristin, in relative silence, he finally brought the vehicle to a stop. In the glare the headlights she could see two horses, saddled and tethered by long ropes to a tree. Nearby were canvas packs.

When Zachary shut off the lights, everything disappeared for a moment. Kristin waited for her eyes to adjust to the moonlight, but her recalcitrant rescuer immediately got out of the Jeep and started moving around in the darkness.

"I don't see why we have to take horses," Kristin reasoned as she lowered herself delicately to the running board and then the ground, "when we have a perfectly good Jeep."

"There are some places," Zachary told her, untying one of the nickering, restless animals, "where only a horse can go." He handed her the reins, and Kristin stood there looking at him, shivering. She hadn't been in the saddle since she was five years old and staying with her mother's parents while Alice and Kenyan put the embassy in order. Her grandfather had taken her for a pony ride at the beach.

Without her having to say she was cold, Zachary brought a fleecy jacket from one of the packs and handed it to her, along with a pair of sturdy boots and heavy socks. Only then did she realize she'd been barefoot through the escape from the palace.

With a little shake of her head, Kristin dropped the reins and sat down on a nearby stump to put on the socks and boots. Between those clodhoppers and her ill-fitting, scratchy cotton pajamas, she'd be a sight.

Zachary snatched back the reins and held them impatiently while she prepared to travel.

"I have to go to the bathroom," she told him sheepishly. She'd never even been to camp, let alone roughed it in a foreign wilderness, and all those trees were giving her the willies.

"Pick a bush," Zachary responded.

Kristin started to protest, then stopped herself. It was clear enough that Zachary still thought she was a spoiled, immature little rich girl, and she wasn't going to give him the satisfaction of showing weakness. "Thank you," she said with dignity, rising to her feet and walking regally across the small clearing.

When she returned, Zachary was waiting to strap a pack on her back.

"What's in this thing?" She frowned as she tried to hoist herself into the saddle, pack and all. The horse sidestepped nervously, and the saddle tipped. The next thing she knew, Kristin was between the animal's legs, and it was prancing in a frantic effort to keep itself upright.

"You been gaining weight lately?" Zachary asked as he caught the horse by the bridle and then soothed it with a pat on the neck.

After scrambling back to her feet, and out of the way of the horse's hooves, Kristin glared at him. "I beg your pardon?"

He shrugged and then made a beckoning gesture. "Come on, I'll help you into the saddle."

Kristin was still insulted. "If you're sure you won't get a hernia from the effort," she replied stiffly.

He laughed. "It may be too late. After all, I just carried you down a rope and up the palace wall." With a sound meant to indicate herculean effort he lifted her into the saddle, and she clung to the pommel with both hands, hoping he wouldn't see how afraid she was.

It didn't help that he swung into his own saddle as easily as a TV cowboy. "Relax, princess," he said, and it was the first kindly tone he'd used since he'd awakened her in the palace. "These animals are hardly more than plow horses. They're not going to hurt you."

Kristin lifted her chin. "I'm aware of that," she lied in a lofty tone of voice.

Zachary chuckled and shook his head, then spurred his horse toward a break in the trees. "Follow me, your ladyship."

Her lips moving in silent mimicry of his remark, Kristin gave her mount a nudge with one heel. "How did you know which room I'd be in back there?" she asked when about fifteen minutes had passed. Even though she didn't like Zachary—indeed, he was the last man in the world she would have wanted to rescue her—she was curious. Besides, five days was too long to keep quiet.

His broad shoulders stiffened in the bright moonlight. "That didn't take a genius—you were about to marry the guy. I looked up an old friend who used to work in the palace, and he sketched the floor plan for me."

Kristin was silent for a few moments, absorbing the fact that Zachary thought she'd been sleeping with Jascha. She didn't know why, but it hurt.

"I did get there before the wedding, didn't I?" he asked, glancing back at her.

Kristin sighed. "Yes. But I wouldn't have gotten married anyway—I'd already told Jascha the ceremony was off."

"I don't think he was convinced," Zachary replied.

She ducked to avoid a low-hanging branch, and her nostrils were filled with the sudden and paradoxical scent of Christmas. "Why not?"

"When I got there you were naked as hell, and you'd been powdered and perfumed for a night of pleasure, that's why."

Kristin blushed, remembering the strange, decadent sensuality of the experience. She'd grown up in Cabriz, but there were a great many things about its culture she didn't understand. After all, she'd always been very sheltered, living within the embassy walls, taking her schooling from a governess. She didn't speak.

Zachary looked back at her again, but the expression on his face was unreadable in the thin moonlight. "They were the Cabrizian equivalent of a harem, princess. It's their job, among other things, to prepare a new bride for their husband's enjoyment."

Kristin had already come to that conclusion, and she was ashamed of her naïveté in believing Jascha when he'd promised she'd be his only wife. "I know that, Zachary," she said quietly. "You can spare me the Cabrizian culture lesson."

He reined in his horse to ride beside her, even though the path was really too narrow. "If you knew, why the hell did you agree to marry the bastard?"

She sighed and ran one hand through her hopelessly tousled hair. "I didn't figure it out until tonight," she confessed, unable to meet Zachary's eyes. "Jascha promised—"

"Jascha promised," Zachary interrupted, and his voice conveyed such contempt that Kristin began to feel defensive.

"He was there for me when I needed him, Zachary," she said evenly.

Zachary glared at her for a moment and she saw the muscles in his throat work, then he rode ahead of her again.

Typical, Kristin thought. Whenever the conversation took a direction Zachary didn't like, he simply clammed up. In all the time they'd been together he'd never told her anything about his childhood or his family, if he had one. All she knew for sure about his past was that he'd never been married and that he'd joined the agency right after he left the air force.

"What if I hadn't wanted to leave Jascha?" she asked.

The path was broader there, but Zachary didn't wait so she could ride beside him. "I wouldn't have forced you," he replied quietly.

"Even though your orders were to bring me back no matter what?"

She saw the broad shoulders tighten under his battered leather coat. "I'm not here under anybody's orders," he answered.

"Not even Dad's?"

Zachary permitted himself a raspy chuckle. "Well, he did offer an opinion."

"I can imagine," Kristin replied ruefully. She and her father were certainly not close—she'd never, to her knowledge, done a single thing that pleased him—but she liked to think the man cared about her, at least a little.

The glimmer of the moon showed a rocky plateau up ahead, followed by another steep incline. "Why did you do it?" Zachary asked hoarsely. "Why did you come over here, when you knew the country was in an uproar? Did you love him that much?"

Kristin bit her lower lip, searching her mind for satisfactory answers. God knew, those were questions she'd asked herself often enough during the past few weeks as the fighting had grown worse and Cabriz's relations with other governments had collapsed. "A year ago, when Jascha and I started seeing each other again, in New York, things weren't so volatile over here. And there was the fairy-tale aspect of it all—we were on the covers of magazines, and Jascha sent flowers every day...." She stopped and glanced at Zachary, trying to read his reaction in the set of his frame, but he gave her no sign of his feelings. "I got swept up into the storybook-princess element of the thing, and it wasn't until I came over here that I began to have doubts."

For a long time the only sounds were those of night creatures prowling the nearby woods and of the horses' hooves on the stony ground. Then the question came again.

"Did you love him?"

Kristin had been stalling, but she still wasn't prepared. "I don't know, Zach."

He didn't reply, and they began the ascent up the side of the mountain. Kristin felt as though the weight of her backpack alone would pull her over the horse's rump and onto the ground.

Finally they reached fairly level ground again. "Where are we going to sleep tonight?" she asked, breathless from the effort of holding on to the pommel of her saddle.

Zachary gave her a sour look. "The Ramada Inn," he answered.

Kristin felt anger swell inside her, but she was too tired, cold, hungry and frightened to give free rein to it, so she just rode quietly until her temper had deflated a little. "There's no need to be snide," she pointed out.

Holding the reins in one gloved hand, he bent in a mocking bow. "I beg your pardon, your ladyship. I'll try to keep a civil tongue in my head from now on."

Tears pressed behind Kristin's eyes and clogged her sinuses, but she held them back. "I haven't had my dinner, you know," she said, keeping her chin high.

Zachary produced something from the pocket of his leather jacket and shoved it at her.

She took the item from him with trembling fingers. It was a candy bar—her favorite combination of chocolate and coconut—and though it was a little squished, it looked like a feast to Kristin. She thanked him, unwrapped it with awkward haste and indulged in a bite.

"Want some?" She felt duty bound to offer, though she hoped Zachary would decline.

He shook his head. "No, thanks. I'll have something when we stop for the night."

So they *were* stopping. Kristin was relieved to hear that. "Umm," she said, enjoying her candy bar.

Zachary spared her a grin. "Did you think I'd forgotten what you like?"

Her throat constricted with unwanted emotion. It was just like him to remind her of old times, when they'd lived together. He'd left her favorite candy on her pillow in those days, or tucked it into her pocket, or hid it in her camera case.

She blinked several times and swallowed hard. "I doubt if you've given me a thought since the day I moved out of your apartment," she said evenly.

They were moving into the trees again, and Zachary rode ahead, forcing Kristin and her horse to fall in behind. He spoke in a terse voice. "Then you're wrong. I've thought about wringing your neck a million times."

Kristin sighed. Despite the jacket Zachary had bundled her into, she was cold, and the candy bar had only taken the edge off her appetite. Worse, she was beginning to consider the reprisals Jascha might use if they were caught. "If you hate me so much, why did you come into Cabriz to get me?"

He didn't look back. "Because I get a kick out of sneaking into countries with names that sound like a line of sportswear," he answered tartly.

"Jascha will kill you if he catches us."

"You'd better pray he doesn't, princess. He's probably not real fond of you right now, either."

Kristin remembered the look on Jascha's face when he'd been about to force himself on her, and she shuddered. "I don't know what's come over him lately. He was always so sweet, and so gentle."

Zachary's tone was wry. "Little things like the overthrow of a throne tend to upset a guy."

Kristin's weary mind had gone on to other possibilities. "What will they do to Jascha—the rebels—if they do overrun the palace?"

He waited a long time to answer, and when he spoke his voice was gruff with reluctance. "They'll kill him, princess."

The grief that surged through Kristin shouldn't have come as a surprise, but it did. Jascha had been her friend, if not her lover, for a very long time. After she'd lost Zachary, the prince had dried her tears and listened patiently while she tried to work out the things that had gone wrong.

Her shoulders hunched under the heavy load of the backpack and tears trickled down her cheeks.

Zachary must have known she was weeping—try as she might, she couldn't seem to cry quietly—but he didn't make any comments. He did take the reins from her and lead her horse behind his.

By the time he brought both horses to a halt in the shelter of a small circle of trees, Kristin had recovered some of her dignity.

She felt abject relief when Zachary reached out, still mounted on his horse, to unfasten and remove her backpack. "I can hardly wait till we get the fire built," she said with a sigh, summoning up a tremulous smile.

He swung down from the saddle, carrying her backpack, and tossed it into the leaves that covered the ground. "No fire tonight, your ladyship," he answered in clipped tones. "We're still too close to Kiri, and there are probably patrols out looking for us right now."

Kristin shivered and glanced around at the woods. They looked eerie in the silver glow of the stars and moon. "Do you really think so? It would make better sense if they started out in the morning."

He shrugged out of his backpack and set it down beside hers. "Right. And if we just follow the yellow brick road, we'll be home in Kansas by morning and Auntie Em will bake us an apple pie."

It was a struggle, but Kristin managed not to lose her composure. She watched as Zachary took the reins of both horses and started off toward the woods, and when it was clear he wasn't going to apologize for patronizing her, she stormed after him.

"Why do you always do that?" she demanded.

"Do what?" Zachary retorted, all innocence. A stream flowed a few yards ahead, shining like a silver ribbon in the night.

"Why do you always make me out to be so damn naive? I happen to have a degree in journalism, you know, and I've been all over the world on professional assignments!"

While the horses drank, Zachary turned to Kristin, his nose less than an inch from hers. "Some assignments—you took pictures of embassy parties and wrote cutesy articles to go along with them. And as for *this* little adventure, you came halfway around the globe to marry a prince who already has half a dozen wives, in a country that's been teetering on the edge of disaster for ten years, and then you have the gall to stand there and ask me why I think you're naive?''

Kristin stepped back, strung, and would have fallen if Zachary hadn't been so quick to reach out and steady her. She blinked, unable to refute the charge that her job with *Savoir Faire* had amounted to little more than writing the occasional society column. ''I didn't know about the wives.''

Zachary let her go. ''In fifteen minutes,'' he said, ''you'll have convinced yourself there were never any wives. Well, you have it your way, your ladyship. You've always arranged the world to suit your perceptions, anyhow. Why should this be any different?''

''You're being cruel, Zachary. I'm not trying to deny that I made a mistake.''

''*A* mistake? Sweetheart, you've made a dozen. Why did you think all those women were hanging around? Did you have them pegged as members of the palace sewing circle?''

Kristin's eyes brimmed with tears and she whirled to walk away, but Zachary reached out and caught hold of her arm, turning her back to face him with surprising gentleness.

''Kristin, I'm sorry,'' he said softly. Unwillingly.

Kristin bit down hard on her lower lip.

Zachary touched her cheek, brushed away a tear with the edge of his thumb. ''Don't cry, princess.''

When Kristin didn't respond, he released her and turned back to the horses. She walked a little way upstream and knelt down to splash clear, icy water onto her face.

It restored her a little, and when she joined Zachary in the clearing she was almost her old self. He tied the horses where they could graze, then knelt beside her and took a bedroll from her backpack.

"It's going to get cold tonight," he said as he zipped his sleeping bag and Kristin's together.

Kristin's eyes widened. "You mean we're sleeping in the same bag?"

Zachary gave her one of his impatient looks. "It's not like we've never shared a bed," he pointed out.

Kristin's mind filled with sweet, fiery and completely unwanted memories at the prospect. "But we're not—we were involved then."

"Relax, your ladyship. I don't intend to touch you."

Chilled, not only by the night wind but by the timbre of Zachary's voice, Kristin shivered. "I'm hungry," she said.

He reached for one of the backpacks again. "I'll get you something. Take your clothes off and get into the sleeping bag."

Kristin had been unlacing one of her clunky hiking boots, but she stopped cold. "You expect me to strip? In your dreams, Zachary Harmon."

Holding a package of something in one hand, he turned his broad and singularly imperious back. "Get undressed," he reiterated. "If you don't, your clothes will draw moisture and you'll end up with pneumonia."

Kristin studied his back, trying to decide whether he was telling the truth or not. "If you're lying to me—"

He turned to face her, tossed the small package into her lap and took off his hat. The moonlight shimmered in his rumpled brown hair. "I've never lied to you in my life," he said. And he unzipped his jacket and laid it aside, then pulled his shirt out of his jeans and began to unbutton it.

Kristin's cheeks felt as though they'd caught fire, and she dropped her eyes. "All right," she said. "I'll take off my clothes. But you have to look the other way until I tell you it's okay."

He turned away in a leisurely fashion, and Kristin heard a slight clinking sound as he unfastened his belt buckle. "Were you this shy with the prince?"

Kristin wasn't about to dignify *that* question with an answer. She took off her hiking boots and socks, then the odd, rough-spun pajamas. Beneath them she was naked, and she practically dived into the double sleeping bag, pulling the top up to her chin and huddling as far as she could to one side.

She squeezed her eyes tightly shut when Zachary slid into the bag beside her, but she could feel the heat of his body, and she was awash in memories of other nights.

"I thought you were hungry," Zachary remarked.

She opened her eyes and felt around on top of the sleeping bag for the packet he'd given her earlier. "I am," she said. The stars seemed to crowd around the moon, determined to outshine it.

Instead of the packet she found rock-hard thigh, which she released instantly.

Zachary laughed. "Here," he said, dangling the packet in front of her face.

Kristin snatched it out of his hand and sat up so rapidly that the sleeping bag nearly slipped down to reveal her bare breasts. She held on to her virtue with one hand and used her teeth to tear open the little bag.

Inside were roasted peanuts, and Kristin gobbled them down, thinking sadly of the spicy, scrumptious meals that were served at the palace.

When she was finished she lay down again. "I wish I could floss."

"Thank you for sharing that," Zachary replied in a sleepy voice.

She resisted a fundamental urge to nestle close to him, not for love but for protection. Her voice was small. "Zachary?"

"Hmm?"

"Are there wild animals in the woods?"

"Umm-hmm."

"Suppose they come after us? I mean, since we don't have a fire or anything—"

Zachary yawned. "Between the two of us, princess, we ought to be able fend off a squirrel attack. Now quit talking and go to sleep—tomorrow's going to be a hard day."

Kristin wriggled farther inside the bag. It was made of some kind of space-age material; although it was thin and light, she was perfectly warm. The ground was a little hard, though. "What do you suppose Jascha's doing right now?"

"Planning our executions. *Go to sleep*, Kristin."

She closed her eyes, but sleep was elusive. Every sound in the woods seemed to be magnified. "I left my camera at the palace," she said with real despair.

Zachary rolled onto his side, turning his back to her. She saw the familiar mole between his shoulder blades and barely resisted the urge to touch it with the tip of one finger.

"Next time I carry you out of a prince's bedroom," he said between yawns, "I'll give you a chance to pack a few things first."

The urge to touch Zachary's mole was replaced by one to give him a kidney punch. "I had taken some very important pictures," she told him, struggling to keep her voice even.

His reply was a theatrical snore.

Kristin rolled onto her stomach in a vain effort to get comfortable, and burrowed down deep into the bag. She fully intended to cry, feeling she had every right after the day she'd put in, but she was too tired. In five seconds she was asleep.

She awakened hours later, in the depths of the night, to find herself cuddled close to Zachary, enfolded in his strong arms. For just a few moments she thought she was back in their apartment, that their breakup had never taken place.

She sighed softly and ran one hand along his muscular thigh; he stirred in his sleep and spread one hand over her bottom, fitting her against him. The size and power of him jolted her back to reality and she jerked away, reaching blindly for her clothes, ready to spend the night sitting bolt upright if it came to that.

But Zachary caught hold of her wrist and stayed her efforts. "You're not going anywhere," he said clearly.

Kristin knew she couldn't fight him; her strength didn't begin to compare with his. If he were to imprison her under his weight and take her, there wouldn't be a thing she could do to stop him.

She was horrified when a thrill of pure lust moved through her, leaving her to shudder in its wake. The words came out of her mouth before she could stop them. "Make love to me, Zachary."

His reply was like a slap in the face. "Not in a million years, princess. I don't travel in your social circles."

Kristin didn't know who she hated more—Zachary for cutting her to emotional ribbons or herself for inviting the intolerable, crushing pain of his rejection. To make her humiliation complete, she began to cry.

"Oh, damn," she sobbed miserably. *"Damn!"*

To her utter surprise, Zachary took her into his arms and held her close. "Go ahead and cry," he said raggedly, his lips moving against her temple. "If anybody's earned the right, it's you."

"I'm not crying because you wouldn't make love to me!" Kristin wailed, clinging to her pride even in the depths of indignity. "Don't you dare think that I am!"

He chuckled and laid a light kiss on her hair. "Whatever you say, princess."

She cried until her grief was spent, her head resting on Zachary's shoulder. Then she hiccuped. "Is there somebody—are you—?"

"No," Zachary answered. "I'm not involved with any particular woman." He patted her bare bottom lightly.

She swallowed. She didn't know why it was important to tell Zachary, but it was. "I never slept with Jascha," she said softly. "In fact, there was never anybody but you."

He didn't reply, and Kristin couldn't decide whether he didn't believe her or he'd fallen asleep again. And she was afraid to find out.

Pure exhaustion rendered her unconscious in the next few moments, and she awakened, hours later, to find herself alone in the sleeping bag. Zachary was up and dressed, and he tossed her another packet the moment she sat up.

"Here's your breakfast," he said cheerfully.

Kristin looked at the packaged food with a baleful expression. "What is it?"

"Dried fruit. Keep your chin up, princess. Tonight we sleep in a cabin, with a real fire on the hearth." He threw Kristin her clothes and calmly led the horses toward the stream.

Three

———

Kristin held on grimly as her horse plodded along behind Zachary's, scaling hillsides so steep that only scrub brush grew there. She would have given her passport for a cup of hot coffee and a powdered sugar doughnut. If she'd still *had* her passport—it was back at the palace, with her camera and journal and other personal possessions.

She tilted her head back, saw that the sky had turned the color of charcoal.

"Aren't we sort of out in the open?" she called after Zachary, mainly to make conversation. She was much too tired to be alarmed.

"Yes," he answered, "so hurry it up."

Resentment simmered in Kristin's cheeks as she spurred the panting horse. After all, *she* hadn't been the one to pick this route. If it had been up to her, they would have left the country in an airliner, or a helicopter at the very least. Before she could frame a retort, however, a blood-freezing *ping* rang in the air.

Zachary yelled something, and Kristin's horse took off at a breakneck pace with no urging from her. She very nearly fell off, and in her mind she saw herself rolling end over end down the slope, backpack and all.

They gained a grassy plateau, with trees, and once he was certain Kristin was safe Zachary leaped off his horse and crept back to the edge of the slope with a formidable pistol grasped in one hand.

"Who are they?" Kristin asked, crawling up beside him as she'd seen soldiers and cowboys do in movies.

Zachary's eyes were narrowed as he surveyed the apparently empty countryside. "Rebels," he speculated with a shrug of one shoulder, "or maybe bandits."

Kristin shivered. "You mean we have to worry about crooks, besides rebels and Jascha's soldiers?"

"Stay back," he growled, still scanning the wooded area at the base of the steep incline they'd just climbed.

"You didn't answer my question."

"Excuse me," was the brusque response as he checked the chamber of the pistol and then produced more bullets from his jacket pocket and thrust them into place with a practiced thumb, "but I'm a little busy at the moment. Maybe we could chat later."

Kristin was about to accuse him of being ridiculous when a second bullet struck the ground not half a dozen feet from where they lay. She scooted closer to Zachary. "I'm scared," she whispered.

"Smart girl," Zachary answered, drawing a bead on something at the edge of the woods. "The good news is, these guys are either lousy shots or they don't want to hit us. We were vulnerable as ducks in a rain barrel while we were climbing the hillside."

Just as Kristin was about to comment, he squeezed the trigger, and the explosion seemed deafening. She covered her ears with both hands and moved closer still to Zachary's side. "Did you hit anything?" she asked, peering toward the trees.

"Probably not. I just want them to know we're prepared to fight back—sometimes that's enough."

"Don't you have binoculars or something?" Kristin queried, watching Zachary squint. She wished she had her camera.

"That would be a great idea, princess," he answered with a long-suffering sigh. "Then they could pinpoint us by the reflection off the glass and blow us to little quivering pieces."

Kristin shuddered. "You don't need to be so graphic."

"Start moving backward, toward the horses," Zachary ordered. "And don't stick that sweet little rear end of yours up in the air. You're liable to get it shot off if you do."

She obeyed, but only because it was a matter of life and death. "I suppose this means we can't have a fire at lunchtime," she lamented as she wriggled along the ground like an earthworm in reverse.

"It means we may not *live* till lunchtime," Zachary replied.

When they were a good thirty feet away from the edge, he rose to a crouching position, one hand splayed on Kristin's back to keep her down. When no shots were fired, he released her.

"Stay as low as you can until you get to the trees," he said.

Kristin was trembling, but she did as she was told. Her clothes were covered with dirt now, and her hair was all atangle around her face. She thought with yearning of her makeup case, and her toothbrush, and a big bathtub filled with steaming, scented water.

Only moments had passed when they mounted their skittish horses, but they seemed like hours to Kristin.

"Ride ahead," Zachary told her.

She knew he was protecting her, but it was little comfort. Surely there were easier, safer ways out of the country. "Are they gone?" she asked. "The people who were shooting at us, I mean?"

"Probably," Zachary answered. But he was obviously on the alert.

At noon they stopped by a stream to water the horses and rest. Zachary produced two more packets of food, this time little pieces of dried meat.

Kristin sat on a log and gobbled down her share, too hungry to complain. "Do they have McDonald's in Rhaos?" she asked as Zachary, having finished his meal, rummaged through his backpack.

He chucked. "Not yet," he answered. "But I'm sure they're working on it." To her wonder and delight he brought out a new toothbrush, still in its box, and a little travel-size tube of toothpaste.

Kristin accepted them eagerly. "I don't suppose you have soap?" she asked in a hopeful voice, kneeling by the clean stream, taking the brush from its package and dipping the bristles in the water.

He grinned. "It just so happens that I do. But you won't need it until later."

Kristin was too busy brushing her teeth to comment. It felt glorious to have her mouth clean and fresh again. When she was finished, she put the toothbrush carefully back into its box and tucked it, along with the tube of paste, into the pocket of her jacket.

"Do you think those guys are still following us?" she asked.

Zachary shrugged. "I don't know. They may have decided we weren't worth the trouble."

"So they probably weren't soldiers."

He shook his head. "No. Soldiers would have surrounded us—probably without firing a shot."

Kristin shook off the horrifying thought. "How do you know they're not going to do that, in an hour, or this afternoon, or tomorrow?"

"I don't," was the blunt reply.

When the horses had rested, eaten a little of the lush grass growing along the stream bank and had their fill of water, Zachary helped Kristin back into the saddle and they set out again. The two of them rode side by side, keeping to the edges of meadows and clearings. Thankfully, they didn't encounter another hillside, but Kristin knew it was only a matter of time.

"I think it's remarkable," she said once in an effort to start some kind of civil interchange with Zachary, "that this part of the country is forested, while the southern section is practically all jungle."

"It's a weird place," Zachary allowed, not so much as glancing in her direction. His eyes moved constantly in this direction and that, like those of a Secret Service agent protecting a high government official.

Not that Kristin thought he had any particular regard for her. He was just doing his job, that was all.

Near nightfall they came to a little hut nestled into the crook of a canyon. The place looked uninhabited, but there was wood piled along one tilting outside wall, and a crooked chimney jutted from the warped roof.

"How did you know about this place?" Kristin asked, getting down from the horse on her own even though she nearly stumbled under the weight of the backpack while doing it.

With a self-confident grin, Zachary unfastened her pack and lifted it away, setting her free. He was standing close, and Kristin felt as though her insides had suddenly been magnetized to his. Her mind gave the command to retreat, but her legs didn't move. She simply stood there, looking up at Zachary and remembering all the times he'd turned her inside out, whether in bed or elsewhere.

He removed his own pack and tossed it aside, his wicked hazel eyes never leaving her face. There was an insolent confidence in his expression but, for the life of her, Kristin could neither move nor speak to thwart him. The old feelings had all come back in force, and it was as though no time at all had passed, as though no wounds had been dealt.

She knew that if he took her then and there, she wouldn't have the strength to object.

It seemed the entire world had shifted to slow motion, with only Kristin's rebellious heart beating a speedy rhythm. Zachary's hands cupped the sides of her face, his thumbs moving gently over her skin. Then he lifted her chin.

She saw his mouth descending toward hers and gave a little whimper, but that was all the protest she could manage. Perhaps, she thought wildly, it had not been a protest at all, but eager submission.

Every subtle injury he'd done her was healed in those moments, at least temporarily, and Kristin would have given her soul to be part of him again.

Everything within Kristin focused on the sensation of his lips touching hers. She felt as if she were standing in a mud puddle, gripping an electric fence with both hands.

His tongue caressed, then parted her lips and boldly explored. Heat surged through her, and her clothes might have been aflame, she was so warm. Her hands ached to tear them off.

He lifted her, without breaking the kiss, and her legs automatically wrapped around his hips, clutching him tightly. This, too, was a part of the familiar pattern between them, one that could have stretched back over other lifetimes besides this one. She could feel the hard promise of his masculinity at the crux of her thighs.

Kristin was trembling when, without warning, Zachary tore his mouth from hers and set her roughly on her feet.

For a moment she was too dazed to react. She just stood there, bewildered, using all her energy to keep from swaying to one side. And when she did manage to speak, all that came out was one word. "Why—?"

He turned away. "I'll take care of the horses," he said, and then he caught hold of both sets of reins and strode off through a copse of trees, leaving Kristin to stare after him in confusion and hurt.

Automatically, her hands rose to her tangled hair. She probably looked a fright, but that didn't explain why Zachary had rebuffed her. She'd felt his passion, burning hot enough to fuse with her own.

Not quite bold enough to brave the hut alone—it looked like the kind of place that would be filled with rats and spiders—Kristin busied herself with her pack instead. Searching through it she found, to her enormous relief, a sturdy comb, the promised soap and another set of clothes, besides packaged food, matches, her sleeping bag and a few first aid supplies.

By the time Zachary returned with the horses, she'd brought her wounded pride under control. She even managed to smile at him as though nothing had happened.

"I guess we're going inside now," she said cheerfully after he'd unsaddled the horses and tied them to separate stakes driven into the ground.

Zachary brushed off his hat and scratched his forehead. His rich brown hair was rumpled and damp with sweat; he needed a bath as badly as Kristin did. "You might have started the fire."

Kristin sighed. "The only fire I've ever started was with those little logs from the supermarket," she reminded him patiently.

There was a distinct chill in the air, since night was approaching, but Zachary's grin warmed her a little. "You're doing all right for a princess," he conceded, picking up her pack and striding toward the door of the hut.

The compliment was strangely sweet, and it found a hiding place in Kristin's heart. "Thanks," she answered, sounding as if she had a frog in her throat.

It was fairly dark inside the hut, since there were no windows to speak of, but Kristin could see cobwebs swaying in the shadows like ghosts, and she had to force herself not to turn and run outside. She wanted to be worthy of the sparse but sincere praise Zachary had given her.

She heard the strike of a match, and then a lone, flickering kerosene lamp lent the place a sickly glow. Suppressing a shudder, Kristin looked around until she spotted a crude homemade broom.

Grabbing it by the handle, she began sweeping down the cobwebs. Darkness still hovered around the ceiling and floor, and Kristin heard tiny clawed feet skittering everywhere. A scream of pure horror rose in her throat when something brushed against her ankle in passing, but she swallowed the cry.

Zachary went outside and returned moments later with an armload of wood, which he dropped in front of a small, strange-looking stove.

"There are probably things living in there," Kristin observed on her way to the door to shake out the makeshift broom.

The door of the stove creaked ominously as Zachary opened it. "They've moved to a better neighborhood," he responded. For a few moments his hands worked mysteriously with the wood, and then a cheerful fire leaped to life.

Kristin felt better immediately. In the temporary illumination, before Zachary closed the stove door, she spotted candles on a rude shelf and appropriated them. Soon after, the place was much more brightly lit.

Unfortunately, that only showed up its many shortcomings.

There was no bed, no sink, no toilet, and there were no tables or chairs. The kerosene lamp sat on an upturned crate marked with Chinese letters.

In one corner a pile of skins, probably crawling with lice and littered with rat leavings, provided the only place to lie down. The floor itself, Kristin could clearly see, was even dirtier, despite the sweeping she'd given it.

"Everything will be all right, princess," Zachary said gently, and she was embarrassed to realize he'd been watching her, reading her cowardice in her face. "I promise."

Kristin hugged herself and ran her tongue quickly over her lips. "I have to go to the bathroom," she said.

"It's out back," Zachary replied, taking cans and small cooking implements from his pack. His gaze was averted now. "Take the broom—you'll probably meet some wildlife."

After drawing a deep breath and ordering herself to have courage, Kristin snatched up the only weapon available to her and marched around back to find a crude privy. The structure was made of very old wood, and it leaned distinctly to the left.

Kristin opened the door and flailed around inside with the broom until she was satisfied that no spider-filled cobwebs would drop onto her head. Something small ran between her feet at the last second, and she screamed.

Zachary was there immediately, but the look in his eyes made her wish she'd encountered a bandit or one of Jascha's soldiers instead of a rat or squirrel. He handed her the flashlight and walked away, and she inspected the inside of the privy thoroughly before stepping in and closing the door.

When she returned to the hut, Zachary was heating water on the stove, along with two tin cans.

Kristin had been to the nearby stream, thanks to Zachary's flashlight, where she had washed her face and hands as best she could. "What's for supper?" she asked.

"Stew," he replied, gesturing toward the pile of skins, which he'd covered with a blanket. "Sit down."

Even before she obeyed, Kristin could feel things crawling on her. "I don't like this place," she said. "Couldn't we just sleep outside?"

"We could," Zachary replied, handing her one of the cans of stew and a spoon. "But it's going to rain like hell tonight, so it wouldn't be very comfortable."

Kristin tried not to think about the things that might be living in the skins beneath the blanket. The stew, at least, was surprisingly good. "Whose place is this?"

Zachary shrugged. "It's been empty as long as I can remember," he answered, taking a place beside her on the blanket and beginning to eat from his own can of stew.

"So you've been here before."

He nodded.

Because she was tired, and dirty, and her hair was a mess, because she'd wanted Zachary so desperately and he'd rebuffed her, Kristin felt a bit testy. "Did it ever occur to you that if you know the place is here, the bandits and rebels probably do, too?"

Zachary's spoon was poised between his mouth and the stew. "Yes," he answered patiently, "it did. But when the sky opens up and dumps the contents of your average reservoir on the countryside tonight, they're going to be holed up somewhere, not out looking for us."

With some difficulty, Kristin got to her feet. Still eating from the can of stew, she made her way to the door, opened it and looked out. Sure enough, there was no sign of the stars and the moon, and the sky was frighteningly dark. Even as she looked up at it, lightning snaked across it like a crack in black glass and the earth shook with the power of the thunder.

Kristin forced the door shut against a sudden and angry wind and turned, with what dignity she could manage, to face Zachary. "It's inhumane to leave those poor horses outside in the storm."

Zachary didn't even stop eating. In fact, he went so far as to talk with his mouth full. "They're in a lean-to."

Again, the very air vibrated with thunder, and particles of dirt sifted down from the roof of the hut. Zachary automatically shielded his can of stew with one hand, but Kristin set hers aside with a thump, all appetite gone.

"This is some rescue," she fretted.

Zachary glared at her. "Don't start," he warned. "Coming here and going through all this just to get your backside out of trouble wasn't high on my priority list, either."

"What was?"

He was chewing. "Wine, women and song."

Kristin was unaccountably stung, and she turned away to hide her feelings. "I need a bath," she announced, just to be saying something.

"Tough," Zachary replied.

She looked around until she found an old wooden bowl that might serve as a basin. Using a little of the water heating on the stove and the sleeve of her shirt, she wiped it out. Then she rummaged through her pack until she found the soap.

"If you wouldn't mind stepping outside—"

Another blast of thunder made the walls of the hut shimmy, and torrential rain battered at the thin roof. "I'm not going anywhere," Zachary replied.

Having set her heart on a bath, Kristin couldn't bear not to have one. She might not get another chance for days.

"Zachary, please."

"I'll turn my back," he conceded, finishing the stew and tossing the can into a corner, where it rattled against other cans from other visits, now rusted.

"I don't trust you."

"You'd better start. Your life depends on it." He grinned and opened his pack, taking out soap and a real washcloth. "All right, you win. I'll just step outside and have a shower. Either you're finished by the time I'm through or you're not. It doesn't make any difference to me."

"Just don't come back in here before I'm dressed."

He arched both eyebrows, one hand on the wooden latch that served as a doorknob. "And if I do?"

"I'll report your behavior to your superiors," Kristin replied out of pure bravado.

Zachary laughed and began removing his clothes, tossing them past her onto the blanket-covered skins. Kristin watched him for a few moments as though mesmerized, then, realizing he'd soon be naked, whirled away.

He laughed again and went outside, into the pounding rain.

Kristin practically ripped off her clothes. Then she poured hot water from the kettle on the stove into the wooden basin and hastily bathed herself from heat to foot. She washed her hair, too, and was purloining a T-shirt from Zachary's pack when she felt a rush of cold, moist air.

Her nipples puckered, not just because of the chill but because she knew Zachary was looking at her. Goose pimples raced over her skin, fast as wildfire.

She wrenched the drab olive T-shirt on over her head and turned to look at him, only to find that he was magnificently naked. She swallowed and, with a great effort of will, turned her head.

"You might have knocked."

"And you might have asked if you could use that T-shirt," Zachary replied philosophically, "so we're even."

She saw the flash of his skin as he bent to take another T-shirt and a pair of shorts from his pack. Kristin noted with despair that they weren't boxer shorts, but the kind that fitted close to his form.

She squeezed her eyes shut.

The next thing she knew, Zachary was zipping the sleeping bags together again and laying them out on the skins. She was only too aware of his tanned, soap-scented skin. It would be cool from a shower in the rain....

"I don't suppose you brought along a deck of cards or anything," she said in a desperate effort to put off lying down beside Zachary, stretching out. Remembering the kiss he'd given her when they arrived, she felt her blood heat and knew she wouldn't be able to trust herself once he'd zipped that bag around them.

He grinned and brought a worn deck from his pack.

"What else do you have in there?" Kristin asked.

"I would have thought you'd know, since you felt free to help yourself to my T-shirt," Zachary responded. Deftly, he shuffled the cards. "I could insist that you give it back, you know."

The shirt carried his scent, even though it was freshly laundered, and Kristin wanted to keep it next to her skin. "I'm too much of a lady to give it to you," she answered evenly, "and you're too much of a gentleman to take it by force."

He sat cross-legged on top of the double sleeping bag, and his chuckle was an evil rasp. "Is that what you think? You *are* naive."

Biting her lower lip, Kristin joined him, carefully arranging the hem of the T-shirt when she crossed her legs. "What's your pleasure?" she asked, referring to the card game.

"Don't ask," Zachary responded, and his eyes moved lazily from her lips to the swell of her breasts to the part of her she most hoped was hidden by the T-shirt.

Kristin flushed. "Stop being such a bastard and tell me what we're playing."

"Strip rummy," Zachary answered, beginning to deal the cards.

Kristin's heart hammered with an emotion that was not entirely made up of dread. There were, if she was to be honest, threads of pleasure woven in, too. That spell that had possessed her earlier was still very much in evidence. "I've never heard of that," she said quietly.

"Every time you lose a hand," Zachary replied knowledgeably, "you have to take off an item of clothing. In your case, it means living on the edge."

Kristin picked up her cards, arranged them, and threw them down again. "I demand a redeal. You cheated."

Using just one hand, he ferreted a flask from a pocket in his canvas backpack. "Now, now, your highness," he scolded, unscrewing the lid of the flask with his teeth. "Don't be a stick-in-the-mud. Sometimes you just have to play the hand you're dealt."

"Okay," Kristin answered, laying out her cards on top of the sleeping bag. "Gin."

Zachary looked at the perfect hand of cards and pulled of his T-shirt, revealing his broad, hairy chest.

Kristin's eyes strayed to the odd little scar beneath his right nipple, the one he'd always refused to explain, then she lifted her gaze to his face. He looked insufferably pleased with himself. "This time I deal," she said, reaching for the cards. She was all too aware that Zachary was wearing nothing now but a pair of skimpy briefs. "Where do you buy your underwear?" she demanded, to let him know she wasn't moved. "In adult bookstores?"

Zachary ignored her sarcasm and offered the flask, which she refused with a shake of her head. He picked up the cards she'd dealt him and arranged them as though the fate of the free world depended on their order. Then, a slow, insufferable grin spread across his face.

"I don't want to play anymore," Kristin announced, flinging down her hand and scrambling into the sleeping bag. By controlling her thoughts, she reasoned, she would be able to forget the filthy skins beneath, and all the things that had probably nested on them.

"Chicken," Zachary responded, pulling his T-shirt back on. He went to the table and blew out the candles and the kerosene lamp, then returned to the makeshift bed by the beam of his flashlight. "You were afraid you'd lose, weren't you?"

"Or win," Kristin answered quite honestly.

He switched off the flashlight and climbed into bed beside her, and the storm outside seemed to shake the very core of the earth. With an exaggerated yawn, he settled in to sleep.

Kristin was afraid to think of what might be outside, sneaking toward them through the storm, and she'd already ruled out contemplation of the things that might be under them. Her mind drifted, as she tried to keep her distance from Zachary, back to another night, when she'd known terror of another kind.

Zachary had been away on one of his mysterious missions when sudden, violent pains had grasped Kristin's insides and wrung a strangled shriek from her throat....

The baby, she'd thought in desperation. Something was wrong with the baby she and Zachary had barely conceived, hadn't even really talked about. Something was terribly wrong.

Stumbling to the phone, doubled over in agony, Kristin had called the paramedics, and they'd arrived in record time—but not soon enough to save the child. She'd lost it on the way to the hospital.

Her doctor had admitted her for a D and C and a night of rest, and the next day Kristin had gone home in a daze of disappointment and grief. Reassuring herself there would be other babies didn't help.

She'd been lying in their bed, alone and sick, when Zachary called. She couldn't tell him the child was gone; that would mean letting go, and she wasn't ready.

But he'd heard the pain in her voice. "Kristin, what's wrong?" he'd demanded. When she didn't answer, he guessed. "Is it the baby?"

She'd remembered the conversations they'd had about babies then, how she'd told him she wasn't ready to be a mother and a wife. And a horrible premonition came over her. "It's gone," she'd answered.

Zachary had been very quiet, and Kristin had known by the questions he asked that he believed she might have gotten rid of their child on purpose, even though he hadn't come right out and accused her of that. And she'd hated him for it.

That very night she'd packed her clothes and left, sending a moving company a few days later for the rest of her things.

Now, lying beside Zachary in the darkness, Kristin was crushed by that same sense of hopelessness. Softly, brokenly, she began to cry, not only for that lost baby but for the lost weeks, hours and minutes, as well. She and Zachary might have found their way through the grief and confusion together, if only they'd tried.

She'd been a fool to run away, and Zachary had been a fool to let her, and now things would never be the same between them again.

Four

___

Kristin felt Zachary's hand come to rest on her shoulder. Gently he turned her over onto her back and, with a thumb, he caressed her cheek.

He didn't ask why she was crying—he was just arrogant enough to assume he knew—and his lips brushed her forehead lightly.

A violent shudder ran through Kristin's exhausted body, and it was as though she'd been thrust back through time, into happier, less complicated days. The barbs they'd exchanged and Zachary's cold looks faded from her memory like golden leaves in autumn.

She wrapped her arms around his neck and snuggled closer to him, needing his warmth and strength.

With a groan, Zachary found her mouth with his own and possessed it fully. Again Kristin was electrified, with nothing to ground her. Her hands moved frantically up and down the muscular expanse of his back, seeking a place to hold on, a way to anchor herself.

He left her mouth to taste her neck, pushing aside her damp hair, and one of his hands closed lightly over her breast. Kristin arched her back and whimpered as he stroked the nipple with the pad of his thumb, causing it to harden in anticipation.

Zachary kissed her again, then went to her breast and boldly took the puckered morsel into his mouth.

Kristin groaned as she felt his tongue circle its prey, cried out when he began to suckle. He brought his hand down over her belly to the fevered mound where her womanhood was hidden, one finger creeping through tangled silk for a preliminary conquering.

While Kristin's bottom rose and fell on the flannel lining of the sleeping bag, her knees falling wide, Zachary treated her other breast to the same thorough loving he'd given the first. Then he began kissing his way lower and lower, and her moist flesh quivered under the passing of his lips.

She pleaded with him, softly, senselessly, and gave a strangled shout of triumphant surrender when he parted the damp curls and took her. Her legs went over his shoulders, her hands flailed wide of her body then raced to his hair.

His strong hand cupped her bottom, holding her high, and she felt his hard back under her heels.

"Zachary," she wailed, and he lashed her lightly with his tongue, rendering her nearly mad with need. Her head flew from side to side, her flesh was wet with perspiration from her hairline to her toes, and outside nature built toward a crescendo to parallel the one Kristin's body strained for.

He gave her two kisses, soft as the touch of a butterfly's wing, and then nipped her gently with his teeth.

She cried out as the torrent broke within her, her body stiffening to align itself with the ferocious flow of pleasure that came from Zachary. She was gasping with exhaustion when he finally lowered her back to the sleeping bag and praying he would give her what she needed most of all, but he wasn't through pleasuring her.

He set her on her knees and brought her down onto the warm moistness of his mouth. His hands reached up to cup her passion-heavy breasts and, while he toyed with her nipples, Kristin writhed on the tip of his tongue, her breathing ragged and harsh.

"Please," she whimpered, "oh, Zachary, please..."

But still he teased her, mercilessly. She danced to the tune measured out by his tongue and lips.

At last, even he could no longer hold back the tide of Kristin's response. She bucked violently as satisfaction overtook her, wringing hoarse, repeated cries from her throat, causing her body to curve into a supple rigidity as everything was demanded of it.

She fell down beside Zachary, convinced she had nothing more to give. But when, after several minutes of slow, tender caresses, he entered her, Kristin's very soul was aflame.

Perhaps because she'd been so thoroughly tamed, she was the first to achieve the pinnacle. She knew immense satisfaction as she used her voice and her hands to guide Zachary through the treacherous territory of his own release, and his gruff cry made her heart catch.

They lay entangled afterward, the sleeping bag twisted around them, their hair and flesh soaked. Outside the little hut the storm continued to rage. Inside, the lovers slept, leaving regrets for the morning.

And Kristin had plenty of regrets when she awakened in the drizzly dawn and remembered.

Zachary, fully dressed, brought her a mug of coffee, made in a small enamel pot on the stove, and kept his eyes averted.

His voice was rough, like the sound of two pieces of rusty metal being rubbed together. "You and the prince weren't planning to have a family right away, were you?"

She knew what he was asking—whether or not she could have gotten pregnant the night before—and she was annoyed by his assumption that birth control was her problem. "No," she said coldly, "I have an IUD."

He turned away, still without looking at her. "The rain's slacked off, and it's a nasty day out all the same."

Kristin squeezed her eyes shut, fighting for control. What was it about this man, that he could injure her so deeply just by what he said or didn't say? "We're moving on, aren't we?" she managed to ask.

"Yeah."

She pulled her pack close and went through it until she found the food packets Zachary—or someone—had put there for her. In one was a biscuit, hard as a hockey puck, in another, dried fruit. She choked the rations down, not because she had any discernible appetite but because she knew she would need all the strength she could garner for the day ahead.

"About last night..." she began. But her voice died away; there were no words.

Zachary tossed the grounds from the coffeepot out the door, rinsed it with water from the kettle he'd apparently refilled at the stream, and flung it into his pack. "Let's not talk about that, okay?"

Kristin felt a surge of anger. That had always been Zachary's stock statement whenever the conversation got too heavy for his liking. She heard echoes from the past.

It bothers you, doesn't it, Zachary, that my social background is so different from yours?

It's not important, Kristin. Let's discuss it some other time....

I think I'm going to have a baby, and I'm really, really scared.

We'll talk about it when I get back from this mission.

When will that be, Zachary?

Soon.

She reached for her pack and pulled out jeans and a T-shirt, the only outfit she had besides the pajamalike garb Zachary had put on her before they left the palace. After a few awkward moments had passed, she was dressed, and she climbed out of the sleeping bag to face him.

"It's interesting that you haven't changed in all this time," she observed, her voice betraying no emotion at all.

Zachary, wearing his jacket and hat, turned slightly to watch as she combed her hair. "What the hell do you mean by that?"

With deft fingers she wove her hair into a French braid and tied it with a tiny piece of string she'd found in the pocket of her jacket. "I mean you still deal with everything you find difficult or distasteful by refusing to talk about it. Don't look now, secret agent man, but that's the coward's way out."

She watched as a muscle tightened in his whisker-bristled cheek, then relaxed again.

"What did you expect, Kristin? A few stanzas of poetry? A declaration of my undying love?"

The words wounded Kristin far more cruelly than she would ever have guessed they could. "No, Zachary," she answered, with a calmness that surprised her. "Not from you."

Outside she tried to saddle her horse, but Zachary said she didn't do it right and elbowed her aside. Her ire simmered and bubbled, but she wouldn't let him see.

"I wouldn't have let you make love to me," she said stiffly once they were mounted, their backpacks in place again, "if I hadn't been so scared. It won't happen again."

He tossed her a cocky grin underlaid with cold steel. "We've got a long way to go before we're out of Cabriz, princess," he replied. "So don't be too sure of yourself."

Kristin wanted to run him down with her horse, but since he was mounted she had to settle for the fantasy. "You are so arrogant!"

He touched the brim of his hat. "Just self-confident," he countered with an obnoxious grin. "You didn't seem to mind my being sure of myself last night, princess."

Her face went crimson. "You go straight to hell, Zachary Harmon. I would have responded that way with *anybody*."

Zachary laughed and reined his horse into the woods, and Kristin had no choice but to follow. Impossible as he was, Zachary was her ticket out of Cabriz, and she wanted desperately to go home.

"Did you ever finish college?" Zachary asked when the hut was well behind them.

The branches of trees hung low over the narrow path in a green arch, filling the crisp morning air with their scent and dripping moisture left from the rainstorm in the night. Kristin ducked. "Yes," she answered in a stony voice. When she and Zachary had lived together, she'd been attending UCLA—the third college in her academic career—finishing up her master's. On more than one occasion he'd accused her of being a professional student.

He glanced back at her with an expression of wry annoyance. "Now, there was an answer abounding with pertinent information. I was thinking about that paper you wrote for one of your journalism classes—'Chauvinists I Have Known,' or something like that."

Kristin couldn't help smiling. "'A Chauvinist's Profile.' It was about you, and I got an A."

"So," he went on, apparently content to ignore the gibe, "once you got your sheepskin, you thought you might as well marry a prince."

"I had a job at *Savoir Faire* magazine," she pointed out in self-defense.

"Did they fire you?"

"No. They sent me all over the world on photojournalism assignments."

"Tracking the diamond-breasted embassy bird, no doubt."

His good-natured contempt hurt, but she was determined not to let him know. "Somebody has to cover those parties," she said.

Before he could make a comment on that statement, which Kristin already regretted wholeheartedly, the sounds of laughter and gunshots rang through the air.

Zachary immediately put up a hand, signaling Kristin to halt and be silent. He took off his hat and put it on again, then spoke in a raspy whisper. "Stay here," he said.

Kristin opened her mouth to protest, then closed it again. Zachary was already moving into the woods on foot, disappearing. She was suddenly terrified that he would be killed or captured, and her heart began to beat so hard that she could practically hear it.

She got off her horse and left it untethered beside Zachary's. Then she made her way through the woods in the direction he'd gone.

She'd traveled only a few yards, catching not so much as a glimpse of him, when suddenly a strong hand reached out and closed over her mouth. An arm encircled her waist and hauled her backward, off her feet.

Thinking of bandits, and of Jascha's revenge, she struggled wildly. Relief and fury clashed inside her when she turned her head and saw that her captor was Zachary.

She glared at him.

"Their camp is about twenty-five yards ahead, through those trees," he breathed into her ear. "Maybe you'd rather I'd just let you stumble right in?"

Kristin's eyes were wide as he set her on her feet and slowly lowered his hand from her mouth. "Bandits?" she whispered, curiously drawn to the noise even though she had the good sense to be properly terrified.

Zachary touched his finger to her lips and gave her a stern look, then started back through the trees, pulling her after him.

"I wanted to get a look at them," she complained once she figured they were a safe distance away.

"You almost got more than a look, princess," Zachary replied through his teeth, fairly hurling her up onto her horse. "You damn near struck up an intimate friendship. Now keep your mouth shut until I tell you it's safe to talk."

She bit down on her lower lip, chagrined but not cowed, and dutifully followed Zachary when he guided his horse in another direction. They'd probably traveled a full two miles before he turned to her and said, "There must have been fifty of them. We're going to have to be extra careful tonight."

Knowing that probably meant no camp fire, and thus no coffee, Kristin was deflated. "What do we have that's worth stealing?"

"Although it's debatable," Zachary replied tautly, glowering at her, "some of them might consider taking *you*. Of course, once it was too late, they'd understand their error, but I'm afraid that wouldn't help you much. Or me."

Kristin sighed. "All right, I'm sorry. I was just trying to help, that's all. I got to thinking what would happen if you were captured—"

"And you were going to save me, right? Listen, princess, just do us both a favor in the future and follow your usual modus operandi—which, of course, is looking after your own skin and letting the devil take the hindmost."

Kristin bit back an angry response and fought to hold in the tears of frustration and pain that burned behind her eyes. She didn't expect Zachary to like her, much less love her, as he once had, but she wasn't prepared for hatred, either. And while she'd known the events of the night before would never lead to anything permanent, she'd hoped civility would be possible.

After all, once they were out of Cabriz, they could go their separate ways and forget they'd ever seen each other.

"I'm sorry, Zachary."

He reined in his horse to ride beside her. "I shouldn't have said what I did," he admitted. "It's just that when I saw you walking past me, headed straight for that nest of vipers, I lost it. I'm sorry, too."

She smiled at him. "Thanks for catching me before I made their acquaintance," she said, relieved to find that they could still talk without going for the psychological jugular.

After riding for several more hours they stopped again to eat more dried fruit and meat. Kristin would have given anything for a cheeseburger deluxe with fries.

In the distance they could see a small village huddled against the mountainside. Industrious Cabrizians in dark clothes milled around the huts, and smoke curled from the chimneys.

"Are they friendly, Kemo Sabe?" Kristin asked, crunching on a dehydrated apricot.

"They were the last time I came through, but things might have changed. I'm going to have a word with them, and I want you to stay here." He glared at her, shaking one finger in a mock threat. "And I mean it—cross me again and I'll take a bamboo switch to your backside!"

There weren't many things Kristin could be certain of where Zachary was concerned, but this was one—he would never lay a hand on her in anger, no matter what she did. "Bamboo grows only in the south," she reminded him, holding back a smile. "But I'll stay put."

His eyes widened and then narrowed, and Kristin knew he was trying to read her. "Really?"

"Yes," she said, clasping her hands together behind her back, now that she'd been relieved of her pack. "Really."

Zachary took his pistol from the holster under his jacket and extended it, butt first. "I'll be back as soon as I can. If anybody gives you any trouble, shoot them."

Kristin's inner smile faded, and she felt the color drain from her face. "I don't know if I could do that," she answered, trying to hand the gun back.

He wouldn't accept it. "Just don't go looking down the barrel," he grumbled, mounting his horse and setting off toward the village. Then he was gone.

With a sigh, Kristin plunked down on a large rock to wait, the pistol dangling between her knees, pointed at the ground. "I just hope I don't have to shoot anybody, that's all," she fretted.

Her horse nickered in response.

A full hour passed before Kristin saw Zachary riding back toward her, and she was embarrassed by the extent of her relief. She'd begun by imagining that the villagers had proved unfriendly, then pictured herself storming the place to save Zachary from a fate worse than death.

She held the hateful pistol wide of her body by two fingers, like something that smelled bad, as Zachary approached.

He dismounted and took it from her with a chuckle and a shake of his head. "Here," he said, tossing a parcel wrapped in some kind of skin into her hands.

"What is it?" Kristin asked, turning the bundle over. There was a low-grade stench coming from the package. "Don't tell me what kind of skin it is," she added quickly. "I don't want to know."

Zachary laughed. "It's nothing worse than what you slept on last night."

Kristin made a face as she unwound the twine that bound the package, rolled it neatly and tucked it into the pocket of her jacket. She might need it later to tie back her hair.

Inside the package was a gossamer yellow robe, of the kind Mai and the other palace women had worn, complete with a veil. The gown was beautiful, but hardly suitable for riding, and Kristin looked at Zachary in confusion.

"In case we run into a situation where you have to pass as a Cabrizian," he said, averting his eyes.

Beneath the robe was a round, curious lump of something hard and white. Kristin's nose wrinkled as she assessed the stuff.

"Cheese," Zachary explained, flipping open his jack-knife and cutting off a wedge. He laid the morsel, still resting on the edge of the blade, to Kristin's lips.

"What kind?" Kristin asked, chewing. For all that it smelled like dirty socks, it wasn't bad.

"You're happier not knowing," he answered, giving her another piece.

After Kristin had packed away the robe and, with considerably less enthusiasm, the cheese, Zachary fastened on her pack again and helped her into the saddle. They headed around the village and up the mountain.

They didn't talk much, and Zachary was on the alert. Maybe it was just that they'd nearly stumbled onto those bandits that morning, but Kristin didn't think so. She figured it was more likely that the villagers had warned him about something.

And she was nervous.

Late that afternoon her horse picked up a stone and started to limp.

Zachary lifted the animal's foreleg and inspected the damage, talking with gruff gentleness to comfort the beast, and Kristin felt an unwanted tenderness rise within her.

She turned away resolutely, her arms folded. She couldn't afford to let herself fall in love with Zachary Harmon again, knowing that he could never feel the same way about her. Maybe, for that matter, he never had.

There were some berries growing at the side of the path and she began to pick them, mostly for something to do. In a glance back over one shoulder, she saw that Zachary was using his jackknife to pry the stone out of the horse's hoof.

She raised one of the purple berries to her lips and ate it, enjoying the tangy sweetness. She followed that with another, and another.

When Zachary had finished doctoring the horse, Kristin strolled back to him and held out her hand. "Berry?" she asked cordially.

He just glanced at the fruit at first, but then his eyes widened and he grabbed Kristin's hand, lifting it so he could get a closer look. He muttered a swearword, wrenched off his hat and hurled it onto the ground.

"What's the matter?" Kristin asked. But even as she uttered the words, a sudden spate of nausea overwhelmed her, sending her scurrying for the bushes. She retched violently, repeatedly, and Zachary stood at her side the whole time, one hand resting on her back.

"They were poison," she managed, once her stomach was empty, and Zachary nodded, handing her a mug filled with spring water.

She rinsed her mouth and spat, then drank. "Am I going to die?" she asked shakily. The joke was awkward. Flat.

"No," Zachary answered seriously, "but for the next few hours you're going to wish you had. Weren't you ever a Girl Scout, princess? You don't go around eating whatever you find growing on a bush, you know—"

Kristin was sick again, and Zachary stood by her until the spasms stopped. Then he helped her onto her horse.

"Just hold on," he told her gently, patting the elderly gray mare on the neck. "The Silver Bullet and I will do the rest."

"But I need to lie down," Kristin fussed. She was never at her best when she was sick. In fact, Zachary always used to say that a simple cold could regress her to the age of five.

Zachary had taken the reins from her. "We've got to keep moving until nightfall, princess," he said reasonably. "There are rebels and robbers all over this mountain."

Kristin's stomach clenched wildly, painfully, even though there was nothing inside it to expel. "Just shoot me, then," she pressed, only half in jest.

They rode until they came to another stream, toward dark, and Kristin was so miserable that she would have fallen out of the saddle if Zachary hadn't lifted her down.

"Can I sleep now?" she asked.

He chuckled and kissed her forehead. "No, princess. Not yet. But the horses need water." He unfastened her pack and then went through his own. Finding his washcloth, he carried it to the stream and dipped it.

He was wringing the cloth out as he walked toward Kristin. "Here," he said quietly, laying it across the back of her neck, under her bedraggled braid. "This ought to help a little." He sat her down on a rock. "Wait here."

Kristin was too woozy to wander off. She couldn't keep her mind on anything except the unceasing pain in her stomach.

When Zachary returned, he was holding something in the palm of his hand. "Close your eyes and open your mouth," he said. "And then swallow."

She was trying to see what it was he was offering her, but he wouldn't permit that. And the awful stomach spasms were getting worse. "What—?"

"Just do as I ask for once, princess."

She drew a deep breath and squeezed her eyes shut. "It's not that cheese, is it? I don't feel like—"

Suddenly her head was pulled back and something cold and slimy slithered into her mouth. She tried to spit, but Zachary caught her lips between his fingers and held them closed.

"Swallow," he ordered.

Kristin did so, having no real choice. "What was that?" she sputtered when he let her go, bolting off the rock.

"It was a raw egg."

Kristin whirled away just in time to keep from throwing up on his boots. But this time was different. After the first spate of sickness, her stomach settled down and she almost felt normal.

"Do you need another egg?"

She gave him a look fit to kill and stomped over to the stream, where she knelt and splashed water over her face and into her mouth. Although she was still dizzy, the violent nausea was gone.

"I suppose I don't want to know what kind of egg that was," she said as Zachary squired her back to her horse, strapped on her backpack and helped her mount.

"You're right," he answered, giving her bottom a little swat before she plopped into the saddle. "You don't want to know."

They rode on and on, it seemed to Kristin, up slopes as steep as the side of a refrigerator, through trees so dense that it was hard to pass between them. She thought with longing of her old chenille bathrobe and a cup of hot, strong tea, but she didn't ask Zachary to stop. Her pride had taken enough of a beating that day.

Finally, when it was not only dark but the moon was riding high in the sky, they reached another canyon, and Zachary instructed her to wait while he rode through the opening.

The minutes that passed before he returned seemed like generations to Kristin, but she waited as she'd been told, grateful that he hadn't left his pistol as well.

"It's clear," he said, returning to the gap in the rock to take off his hat and lean slightly forward in the saddle. "Come on in, princess. This is the closest thing you're going to get to luxury accommodations."

With a slight frown, Kristin rode through the breach and looked around.

The moon seemed to be pouring its light into the canyon, where it collected in a silver glow. A spring or stream rippled in the background, but there were only a few trees.

Kristin took off her pack on her own, once Zachary had lifted her to the ground, and headed straight for the water. There was something strange about it, though she couldn't quite decide what it was.

When she reached the pebble-strewn banks of the spring, she knew. It was as hot as bathwater, and steam billowed off the surface.

She whirled, full of weary delight. "We can stay—can't we? We can spend the night here?"

He came to her, kissed her lightly on the forehead. "We can spend the night here," he confirmed. "Go ahead and get a bath. I'll build a fire and see what I can rustle up for supper."

Kristin's eyes went wide as she looked at the spring again. "There wouldn't be any leeches, or anything like that—"

Zachary shook his head, grinning.

With a little whoop of joy, Kristin shed her jacket and bent to untie her work shoes. Only then did she remember that she had an audience. "You'll turn your back, of course?"

Zachary was still grinning. "Of course," he answered.

She took from her pack the robe he'd gotten her that day, along with a bar of soap, and made her way to the edge of the spring. Once she'd taken off her jeans and T-shirt and climbed into the water, she looked back and found Zachary standing in exactly the same place she'd left him, staring at her.

"You lied," she called, but she couldn't work up any real anger. Not when he'd done his best to look after her and had brought her to a place like this.

She was mildly disappointed when he didn't offer a comeback but simply turned and started gathering twigs for a fire.

Kristin settled into the luscious water, soap in hand, and began to bathe.

Five

―――――

I thought we weren't going to have a fire," Kristin said, combing the tangles from her clean, wet hair as she approached Zachary. "Because of bandits and rebels and bogeymen."

He was crouching beside the small blaze, and his eyes wandered over Kristin's gauzy yellow robe for several moments before rising to her face. "The campsite is sheltered by the canyon walls," he pointed out, his expression solemn.

Kristin glanced uneasily around her. The place was too perfect, too much like Eden or Shangri-la. There had to be a serpent somewhere, waiting to offer her an apple. "If you know about it, they probably do, too. And tonight there isn't any rain to keep them away."

Zachary bent to take his miniature coffeepot from the coals of the fire and pour the contents into their mugs. He held one out to Kristin as he sipped from the other, then lowered it slowly from his mouth. "We're as safe here as we would be anywhere else on the mountain," he responded.

"Which isn't saying much," Kristin speculated, hugging herself with one arm and tasting her coffee. "Maybe we should just have kept moving."

"You've been sick most of the day," Zachary reminded her. "And you're not used to this kind of life. You couldn't have gone much farther."

Kristin took another sip of the coffee. Even though there were grounds floating in it, since Zachary always made the brew without benefit of basket or filter, it was delicious. "I should have asked you about those berries before I ate them," she confessed with a sigh. "I'm sorry. This trip is difficult enough without my complicating it."

He approached her, kissed her lightly on the forehead. "It was an innocent mistake," he said. And then he set his coffee mug down and ambled toward the spring, where Kristin had taken such a luxurious bath.

She watched him toss his hat aside, shrug out of his jacket, kick off his boots. Then, realizing that she was staring, Kristin looked purposefully away.

"How many more days until we're out of Cabriz?" she called, her voice unnaturally loud even considering the distance between them.

"Three," he answered. "Two if we're lucky." She heard a splashing sound and envisioned him washing his hair.

She poured the dregs from the coffeepot into her cup. "And then?"

"And then we'll go our separate ways," he replied easily. "You'll probably want to spend a little time recuperating at the embassy in Rhaos. You can look now, Kristin—I'm not exposing any relevant parts of my anatomy."

She realized how tense she was—silly, really, after giving herself to this man so completely the night before—and made a diligent effort to relax. She even strolled toward the spring and sat down on a log. The truce between them was comforting, and she wanted to maintain it. "You haven't told me anything about your life. How's the spy business these days—rescuing former roommates aside?"

He had rinsed his hair and was soaping his armpits, the water reaching to his rib cage. "I wouldn't know," he answered. "I've been teaching at a junior college on the Washington coast ever since . . . well, for the last year and a half."

He'd been about to say, "since we broke up," Kristin knew. The reminder hurt, and so did the knowledge that he'd resigned from the agency. Before their parting she'd begged him to do that so they could build some kind of sane life together, and he'd steadfastly refused.

"You're teaching," she said in a small voice. "What's your subject? Survival in the wild? Covert operations?"

In the thin light of the moon she saw his lips twist into an expression that might have been either a grimace or a smile. "Political science," he answered. "I also do the occasional seminar on Asian culture."

Kristin scraped her lower lip with her teeth. "I'm surprised," she said evenly, still grappling with the unexpected pain. "I wouldn't have thought you'd ever want to do anything as tame as teaching." She wouldn't have thought he'd reveal so much about himself so easily, either. She wondered if it was too much to hope that Zachary was loosening up a little.

He was splashing away the lather from his chest and underarms. "People change, princess," he said. And then she felt his eyes move over her, assessing, finding her wanting. "At least, some of us do."

And here she'd been thinking charitable thoughts about him. "What's that supposed to mean?"

"You're still impulsive," he said in a totally objective tone of voice. "And you still can't make up your mind what you want to do with your life. You go to this college, you go to that college. You take a job, then you give it up to marry a prince. After that, you decide maybe that isn't such a good idea...."

Kristin's cheeks were hot. She started to speak, then stopped herself. It galled her that she couldn't deny Zachary's charges.

"You seem to have a serious problem with commitment," he finished. "Maybe you ought to get some counseling or something."

Kristin gave an angry hoot. "That's a good one, coming from you! If I remember correctly, you were the one who didn't want to be 'tied down' to an everyday job—"

He stalked out of the hot spring before Kristin had a chance to prepare herself and stood there before her, gloriously naked, glistening with mineral water and moonlight. Reaching down, he caught hold of her robe and wrenched her to her feet. "My life is in order," he said in a ragged, angry whisper. "But you're still running, aren't you?"

Kristin tried to pull away, but his hold was too firm. "Running? I was practically abducted!"

"Abducted, hell. You could have stayed in the palace if you'd wanted to and you damn well know it."

She whirled, and this time he let her go. When she looked at him again he was dressed, except for his jacket, hat and boots. He used her comb, then tossed it back to her, and there was a dismissal in the gesture that stung Kristin to the quick.

She busied herself looking through her pack for something to eat that hadn't been dried, and came up with a small can of chicken and noodles with a pop-up lid.

"Do you regret leaving him?" Zachary asked, and her hand tightened around the can.

"Jascha?" Kristin paused, considering. "Yes, in a way. I miss the man I thought he was." She opened her supper and set the can carefully in the embers to heat.

There was an awkward silence, then Zachary said, "I saw your picture on the cover of that magazine."

The engagement photograph of her and Jascha. He'd worn his official uniform for the shoot, and someone had found a rhinestone tiara for her. Kristin smiled sadly, mourning the pretty dream.

"You looked like a real princess," Zachary added, and his voice was hoarse.

She raised her eyes to his face, wondering what he'd thought and felt, looking at that picture. Had there been any pain, any remorse for all the two of them had lost? "Thanks—I think."

He grinned, strapping on his shoulder holster, then busied himself for a few minutes wiping down the barrel, cleaning the chamber. Then he spun the chamber once with an expert thumb. "Your noodles are about to burn," he pointed out.

Disappointed, yet not knowing what she'd expected from him or even hoped for, Kristin carefully removed the can from the fire, using the T-shirt she'd worn that day as a pot holder. "Expecting trouble?" she asked, spooning a bite of food into her mouth and nodding toward the pistol. The noodles tasted smoky and good.

Zachary shrugged, pulling on his jacket. "It wouldn't hurt to have a look around," he answered, then he raised a finger. "And Kristin—"

"I know, I know," she interrupted. "Stay here."

She told herself it didn't make her nervous, having Zachary leave her alone in camp. She finished her supper, disposed of the can and washed her spoon in the spring.

Then, because Zachary still wasn't back and inactivity was unbearable, she took out her sleeping bag and unrolled it next to the blaze. Tonight, with the fire and the warm spring nearby, there wouldn't be any need for them to sleep together.

By the time she'd finished the task, Zachary still hadn't returned.

Kristin brought out her toothbrush and paste and attended to her teeth, using water from Zachary's canteen in lieu of going to the spring. After that there was nothing more to do.

Kristin looked at the high, invisible walls of the canyon, at the V of stars visible in the cleft overhead. Zachary was probably right, she concluded. They were as safe there as they would be anywhere on the mountain—which meant they were in mortal danger at every moment.

Telling herself to be brave, Kristin pulled back the top of her sleeping bag and climbed in, still wearing the yellow robe. It was soft and comfortable, and it made her feel a whole lot less vulnerable than she had in Zachary's T-shirt.

She had just snuggled down, her eyes on the hypnotic, dancing flames of the camp fire, when Zachary returned. She was so glad to see him that she sat bolt upright and blurted out, "Did you see anybody?"

"No," he answered with a sigh, taking in the single sleeping bag without a noticeable reaction, "but that doesn't mean a damn thing."

"Maybe one of us had better sit up and keep watch," she ventured.

Zachary grinned and took off his hat and jacket. The firelight gleamed on the pearl handle of the pistol. "Good idea. If anybody comes into camp, princess, you just interview them. Promise them a spot in *People* magazine.''

"Funny," Kristin replied, swallowing. Something had been troubling her all evening, just beneath the surface of consciousness, and now it bobbed to the top with brisk clarity. "If you're not with the agency anymore, what are you doing here in Cabriz?''

In the dim light of the fire and the moon, Kristin couldn't read Zachary's expression. He was a long time answering. "I have a specialized knowledge of the country," he finally said. "You know that.''

A tiny flame of crazy optimism flared in Kristin's heart, and it made her bold. "And no one else does?''

He drew nearer, crouching beside her, taking her chin roughly in hand. All hope died when she saw the cold expression in his eyes. "The current administration probably would have left you here if it hadn't been for me," he said. "Their reasoning was, 'she made her bed, let her sleep in it.' And under any other circumstances, I would have agreed with them.''

Kristin felt painful venom spread through her veins, made up of shame, frustration and pain. She looked away, and Zachary finally let go of her chin. She lay down and turned her face toward the darkness so he wouldn't know how much she was hurting.

It came as a total surprise when she felt her sleeping bag being unzipped. She sat up, her heart hammering. "What are you doing?''

He attached his bag to hers with such practiced deftness that Kristin was filled with searing jealousy, imagining him lying in such close quarters with another woman. "I think that's fairly obvious," he answered, kicking off his boots.

"You're not sleeping with me!''

"You're right. I don't plan on sleeping.''

Kristin was furious, not because she thought Zachary would force her but because she knew he could change her mind in the space of one kiss. She started to scoot backward, out of the sleeping bag, but that only made the robe bunch up around her thighs.

He unbuckled the holster and set it carefully aside, and before she could pull down the hem of her robe he was lifting it over her head, tossing it aside in a billowing cloud of softness. She was naked, shivering in the heat of his gaze.

"Stand up," he said quietly. "I want to look at you."

Kristin shook her head, already falling under his spell, using all her strength to break the enchantment. "No."

He reached out, cupped her breast gently in one hand. The nipple went taut as he stroked it, and Kristin gave a little moan and let her head fall back.

Zachary chuckled and leaned forward to drink languidly from her breast, and in that moment she was lost. Try though she did, she couldn't summon the words to put him away from her.

Once he'd taken nectar from both her nipples, he again asked her to stand, and this time Kristin complied.

She trembled, knowing what was coming, and made a soft whimpering sound as he parted the silken veil to taste her. "Zachary—"

He teased her with nibbles, with darting flicks of his tongue. "What?"

Kristin moaned. She was exhausted from riding all day; every muscle in her body ached. And yet a treacherous energy was gaining strength within her, holding her up for Zachary's pleasure and her own. Her fingers were entangled in his hair. "I want it to happen when you're inside me. Please."

To her surprise, he lowered her to the sleeping bag, laid her gently on the flannel. The backs of her knees rested against his shoulders while he opened his pants.

He found the velvet passageway and entered with a forceful thrust, his hands gripping Kristin's ankles as she arched her body to receive him.

"That's good," she whispered. "So good—"

Zachary took her fully, then retreated almost to the point of withdrawal. His chuckle was raw with any emotion but humor. "And tomorrow—you'll say you would have responded the same way—to anybody."

"No one," Kristin half sobbed, because the pleasure was already too much for her. She couldn't bear it. "No one else—oh, Zachary, fast—hard—"

He didn't change his pace at all. He held her legs where they were and moved in and out of her with excruciating slowness.

She tried to writhe but he wouldn't permit that, either. He glided in and withdrew and she felt the friction in every nerve, and gloried in it.

Kristin arched her neck and groaned through clenched teeth. "Please."

"No," he answered, pushing her legs forward slightly so that his penetration was deep.

The stars blurred against the dark sky as Kristin climbed toward them, hand over hand, her breathing fast and harsh. Her feet rested against the sides of Zachary's head now, and he held her tightly around the thighs, moving with more speed as his own body began to make demands that would not be ignored.

With a broken cry, he slammed deep and stiffened against her, and in that moment Kristin went wild. She was a woman untouched by civilization, and she was not simply making love—she was mating for life.

Later, when she lay still in Zachary's arms and the last aftershocks had finally subsided, she faced facts. Although what had just happened was of profound significance to her, there was no reason to think anything had changed for Zachary.

She turned her face into the bare flesh of his shoulder, holding back weary tears, and a tremor moved through her.

In response, Zachary held her closer, pulling the top of the sleeping bag up so that it covered them both comfortably. "Cold?"

Kristin shook her head. "Scared." She couldn't add that it wasn't Jascha, or the rebels, or even the bandits that frightened her. It was the thought of going back to a life that didn't include Zachary and trying to pretend seeing him again hadn't awakened all the old feelings.

He kissed her lightly on the temple, his breath ruffling her hair. "In a way," he said, "I'm going to be sorry when this is over."

Kristin closed her eyes tightly so she couldn't cry. She didn't answer, not daring to speak.

Somehow, Zachary seemed to know that she needed holding as much or more than she'd needed his lovemaking. He kept her tucked close to his side long after he'd drifted off to sleep. And even though she was wide awake, Kristin dreamed.

She dreamed of being married to Zachary, and of bearing his children, and of finally making a real place for herself in the scheme of things. She saw herself taking pictures for a newspaper and writing about things that really mattered.

Because she was so caught up in her thoughts, she was startled when Zachary suddenly stiffened beside her and then groped for the pistol.

A strange voice came out of the darkness, speaking in swift Cabrizian dialect, and Kristin caught enough of the general meaning to be terrified.

"Leave the gun where it is and you won't get hurt."

The horses nickered and fretted in the darkness, and Kristin finally picked out the figure of a small man standing on the other side of the dying camp fire and pointing a rifle at them.

Zachary's body was perfectly still, his words evenly modulated. "Who are you?" he asked in the robber's own language.

"We need horses," the bandit replied, and it became obvious to Kristin that he was nervous. "We won't take the woman, we won't take the food. Just the horses."

"No," Zachary said as forcefully as if he had a choice in the matter. "The horses are ours. Leave them here."

The man was insane as far as Kristin was concerned. Why else would he talk that way to someone who was holding a gun on him? "Go ahead," she said in the halting dialect she remembered from embassy days. "Take the horses. Just so nobody gets hurt."

Zachary's elbow landed in the middle of her stomach, just hard enough to cut off her wind.

The bandit came close enough to kick Zachary's pistol out of reach, then backed out of the firelight. Moments later the clip-clop of hooves was heard as the horses were taken away.

Zachary spat a swearword and scrambled out of the sleeping bag, searching the ground for his pistol. By the time he found it, the horses and the bandit were long gone.

And Zachary took his frustration out on Kristin. "I ought to drag you out of that sleeping bag and blister your backside!" he yelled.

Kristin shimmied out on her own and quickly pulled on the yellow robe, as though that could offer some protection. "What did I do wrong?"

"What did I do wrong?" Zachary mimicked furiously. "You drew his attention, for one thing. You should have kept your mouth shut!"

"That wouldn't have stopped him from stealing the horses," Kristin replied reasonably, folding her arms. "Do you think he was alone?"

"Probably not," Zachary answered, picking up his shoulder holster and jamming the pistol inside.

"I told you one of us should have kept watch."

"Right." Zachary was putting on his clothes in jerky, outraged motions. "I can see it now. You probably would have invited them for coffee and asked them if they wouldn't like to steal our food and sleeping bags, as well as our horses. Then we could have been totally annihilated, instead of just in the biggest damn trouble of our lives!"

Kristin stirred the fire and added a few of the twigs and broken branches Zachary had gathered earlier. "Don't you dare try to foist the responsibility off on me—it isn't my fault we were bested by one skinny little bandit!"

Zachary glared at her for a long moment, then startled her completely by chuckling. "He was skinny, wasn't he? If this ever gets back to the guys in the agency, I'll never live it down."

Kristin's concerns were more immediate. "What are we going to do now, Zachary?"

"Sleep," he answered with a deep sigh. "Tomorrow we walk."

"Carrying our packs?"

"That's the idea."

She got back into the sleeping bag, still wearing the robe, and snuggled down. "Do we have enough food?"

Zachary didn't join her, but sat up beside the fire, staring ponderously into the flames. "Probably not," he replied. "Get some rest, princess. Tomorrow is going to be a long day."

He was right.

In the morning Kristin washed up in the spring and dressed in the blue jeans and T-shirt she'd worn the day before, then drank a cup of Zachary's camp-fire coffee. She had no appetite for breakfast, given the situation and yesterday's berry binge.

At first, hiking with a loaded pack on her back was a novelty, and Kristin enjoyed it. It just went to show that all those people who thought she was nothing more than a social butterfly—Zachary and her father, for instance—were dead wrong. Inside her slender form lurked the spirit of an intrepid adventurer.

Then they started traveling uphill.

After advancing only about a hundred yards up the incline, Kristin sank onto a fallen log and covered her eyes with both palms.

Zachary had gone some distance before he realized she wasn't behind him, and stopped. "What's the matter?" he called back, sounding for all the world like a big brother forced to let a small and helpless child tag along on an important mission.

Kristin struggled ingloriously to her feet, almost unbalanced by the pack. "Nothing," she returned with stubborn good cheer. "I just wanted to take a little breather, that's all."

"We've got to keep moving," Zachary replied. And then he turned and went on, and Kristin had no choice but to trudge after him.

The next challenge was a narrow path leading around the edge of a steep slope.

The last of Kristin's bravado teetered on the edge of extinction as she looked down the rocky grade to a pile of mean-looking boulders about a hundred feet below. The path seemed inadequate to say the least—it was hardly more than a line drawn in the dirt—and the weight of two people was sure to send it sliding downhill.

Zachary must have seen the fear in her face, because he laid one hand gently on her shoulder and said, "It's okay, princess. Just hold on to the back of my belt until I tell you to let go, and don't look down."

Kristin drew a deep breath and let it out again. She couldn't fold now, when the time element was even more important than before. With a trembling hand, she reached out and clasped Zachary's belt.

They began to edge slowly along the narrow path, and Kristin looked neither right nor left, up nor down. She just fixed her gaze on the back of Zachary's head, where the hair on his nape curled against the tanned flesh of his neck, and moved as he did.

For all her careful obedience, something went wrong. She set her right foot down and the path fell away beneath it.

With a shriek, Kristin went over the edge, still clinging to Zachary's belt, both feet flailing in an effort to find solid ground.

How he kept his balance Kristin would never know, but Zachary managed to turn and grasp her arm and somehow get her back onto the path.

"Are you all right?" he asked when she was beside him again, face pressed to the rock wall above the ledge, eyes squeezed shut as she battled down the lingering terror.

"My knee," she whispered. "I hurt my knee."

Zachary reached around her, unfastening the backpack. "Okay, Kristin," he said in a reasonable, steady tone of voice, "listen to me. I want you to stay right here while I take your pack to the other side. Once I've gotten rid of it, I'll come back and help you go the rest of the way. All right?"

Kristin swallowed, still afraid to open her eyes. If she so much as glanced down and saw those huge boulders below, waiting to smash her bones, she'd panic and then everything would be lost. "All right." She felt relief as the weight of the backpack was removed.

"Don't try to move," Zachary reminded her, and she could hear the distance growing between them, even though she dared not look. Pure fear rushed into her throat, scalding and vile. "I'll be back in a minute, Kristin. I promise."

Sweat trickled between Kristin's shoulder blades and breasts, and the pain in her right knee intensified. Somehow, when trying to break her fall, she'd twisted it. "Please hurry," she whispered, having no hope that he was close enough to hear.

But he was. "One minute, Kris."

Struggling not to lose her tenuous grip on composure, Kristin nodded and began to count slowly, silently, to sixty.

She felt Zachary's heat and strength just as she reached fifty-seven.

"How's the knee? Can you walk?"

Kristin tested the idea and felt stabbing pain, but she nodded. "I can make it if you'll help me."

His hand rested, firm and strong and very reassuring, on the small of her back. "Just one step at a time, babe—that's all you have to do. I'll be right here to keep you from falling."

Their progress seemed impossibly slow to Kristin, who finally dared to open her eyes but could look nowhere but at Zachary's face. Finally, though, after several minutes, they reached a grassy plateau on the other side.

There Kristin collapsed, engulfed in pain and relief, and sat clasping her knee.

Zachary knelt beside her and gently felt the injured limb, looking for obvious injury. "I don't think anything's broken," he said softly.

Kristin leaned forward and let her forehead rest against his shoulder. The pain was starting to subside, but she didn't have the breath to say so yet.

He put his arms around her, kissed the top of her head. "It's okay, princess. We'll rest until you're ready to move on."

Kristin nodded, and he released her to go and rummage through his backpack. When he returned, he thrust a little package of half-crumpled cookies into her hand.

"I was saving these for the last night, but I think you need them now," he said.

Kristin looked at the treat in disbelief for a few moments, then laughed and wiped her dirty, sweaty face with the back of one hand. "You've been holding out on me!"

He grinned and opened the package for her. "Didn't you tell me once that when you were hurt you used to go to the kitchen for a medicinal cookie?"

Kristin sank her teeth into her lower lip, touched, afraid she'd cry and spoil all her efforts at being brave. Since she didn't trust herself to speak, she just nodded.

Zachary took the only cookie that hadn't broken from the rigors of the trip and touched its edge lightly against Kristin's mouth.

Six

I'm all right," Kristin insisted, running one hand over her sore knee. At least it had stopped throbbing. "I just pulled a few muscles, that's all."

Zachary smiled, still kneeling beside her, brushed the cookie crumbs from her lips and rose to his feet. "Let's see if you can walk," he said, offering Kristin his hand.

She took it and allowed him to pull her up. A shaft of pain shot from her injured knee up her thigh, and she grimaced, turning her face so Zachary wouldn't see. Her first step was sheer agony, but then she took another and another.

A memory flashed into her mind: she was seven, and she'd fallen from the embassy banister and broken her arm. She heard her father's clipped, impatient voice. *Stop sniveling, Kristin. It's your own fault that you fell.*

She held her chin high. "I can make it," she told Zachary quietly.

Zachary caught her chin in his hand and made her look at him. "You can barely stand," he countered, reading the expression in her eyes. For good or ill, he'd always been a master at that.

Stubbornly, Kristin reached for her pack and moved to sling it into place, only to have Zachary take it away again.

"Sit down before you collapse," he ordered tersely, and his manner was nothing short of cantankerous.

"Thanks for the concern," Kristin retorted, "but we can't stay here. You know that as well as I do."

"So have it your way!" Zachary hissed through his teeth. Then he grumbled, "Come on," and set off across the plateau.

Kristin limped along behind him, her teeth sunk into her lower lip, but when Zachary glanced back at her she was ready with a smile and a firm gait.

Grudgingly he moved on, leading the way through thick pine and fir trees. The ground was uneven, but at least they weren't climbing. Kristin didn't know if she could maintain the charade on an incline, even without her pack.

By noon, when Zachary stopped, the pain in Kristin's knee was only a dull ache, but it had sapped her strength, and she knew she was pale.

While she sat on the ground eating cold corned beef from a can Zachary had given her, he paced, agitated and watchful.

"Are we being followed?" Kristin asked, chewing.

"No," Zachary answered, standing on a high ledge and looking down over the mountain they'd been climbing for almost three days. "But I think I see our horses."

Kristin bolted to her feet, wincing at the resultant pang in her knee. "What? Where?"

He pulled a small pair of field glasses from the pocket of his leather jacket and, after checking the position of the sun, peered into them, squinting. "At the edge of that village down there. Looks like our horse thief is a hometown boy."

"What are we going to do?" Kristin asked, following Zachary as he turned away from the ledge with a thoughtful frown on his face.

"*We're* not going to do anything," he said without looking at her.

"Zachary," Kristin warned, staying doggedly at his side as he shed his pack, took the pistol from its holster and checked the chamber. "I'm not staying here by myself."

"Yes, you are," he answered without missing a beat or even bothering to look at her. "You'll lie down, and you'll rest, and when I come back I'll bring the horses with me."

"I want to go."

"And I want the Noble Peace Prize," Zachary informed her. "Guess we're both out of luck, princess." With that, he kissed her on the forehead and started to walk away.

"What if some bandits come and attack me?" Kristin called, hurrying after him, forgetting to hide her limp.

He turned briefly and glared at her with such ominous intensity that she stopped in her tracks. "Ask them what their sign is," he replied, spreading his hands. "Make small talk."

"Zachary!"

He was leaving her again. "If you keep yelling, princess," he warned good-naturedly, "they're bound to find us."

Kristin sank despondently onto the ground. There was no way she could keep up with Zachary's long strides; even without a sore knee it would have been difficult.

She watched him until he disappeared into the trees, then got up and went back to the vantage point at the ledge. All she could see of the village were specks that might have been the roofs of huts and a haze of smoke against the sky.

Kristin ran the tip of her tongue over dry lips and prayed that Zachary would return safely, with or without the horses.

Now that he wasn't there to see, there was no point in trying to pretend she wasn't a physical wreck. Kristin collapsed on the cushiony grass of the plateau, drinking in the thin warmth of the sunshine.

It was inevitable that she would remember the tender moments she and Zachary had shared, there in Cabriz and back in California, where they'd lived together.

The ache in Kristin's heart was worse than the one in her knee. To escape it she drifted backward in time, to a party her parents had given in their home in Williamsburg, Virginia. . . .

The ballroom of the mansion glittered. The women wore dresses as jewel bright as the lights on the towering white Christmas tree in the entryway, and the men were elegant in tailored tuxedos. A string quartet played Mozart, a fire blazed on the hearth and snow drifted past the windows in huge, swirling flakes.

And all the atmosphere was lost on Kristin, who shared a dutiful dance with every man who asked and kept one eye on the big double doorway the whole time. Zachary had promised to spend Christmas with her, but so far there had been no sign of him—and no telephone calls, either.

Instead of visions of sugarplums, Kristin was seeing crashed helicopters and sprays of dust raised by machine-gun fire splattering some dusty Middle Eastern road. Normally she didn't allow herself to think about the things Zachary might be doing when he was away on a mission, but that night she couldn't seem to help it.

She managed a shaky smile when her father, a tall, fit man with a full head of gray hair and shrewd blue eyes, cut in on her bewildered dance partner and took her into his arms for a waltz.

"You look beautiful tonight," Kenyan Meyers told her brusquely, and there was no love in his voice, despite the compliment. "But you're a bit on the pale side. What's the matter? Worried about your soldier of fortune?"

Kristin ached inside. Just once she'd like to feel that her father really cared about her, that she didn't have to put out an effort to win even the most cursory acceptance. She nodded. "Dad, what if Zachary's been shot—or captured?"

Kenyan was annoyed. "Do you see what this relationship is doing to you, Kristin? There are too many uncertainties, too many grim possibilities. Surely you realize that you're headed toward emotional disaster?"

Although she knew her father was probably right, that she should give Zachary up before the fear of what might happen to him made her crazy, Kristin hadn't been able to walk away.

It wasn't that she couldn't live without Zachary—she knew she could. But life would be a flat and endless round of classes and parties without him. "I love him," she answered simply.

Just then, as though the words had conjured him, Zachary appeared in the doorway. His glossy brown hair was dusted in snowflakes, and his eyes searched the long, crowded room for Kristin.

Her heart leaped and, as always, all thoughts of making her way through the world without him dissipated like vapor.

As the dance ended, she stood on tiptoe to kiss her father's cheek, then swept toward the doors, her white lace ball gown whispering as she walked.

Zachary's eyes lit up when he saw her, and one side of his mouth lifted in a smile. He looked uncomfortable in formal clothes, and yet he was the most attractive man in the room.

Catching Kristin's hands in his, he pulled her through the doorway and into the limited privacy of the entryway.

There Kristin flung her arms around his neck, and he picked her up and swung her around once. And then he kissed her.

It was the way it always was when they'd been apart. Kristin suffered a sweet form of cardiac arrest, and all her carefully cultivated gentility deserted her. She took Zachary's hand when the kiss ended and pulled him up the stairs and into the library, carefully locking the door behind them.

The room was lit only by outdoor lights shining through the ever-increasing flurries, but Kristin could see the admiration in Zachary's eyes as he held her at arm's length, taking in her extravagant white dress.

"You look," he said hoarsely, "like a snow fairy."

She smiled, and the music from the ballroom seeped through the venerable floors. "I'll have this dance, if you please."

He grinned, and her heart turned over, as it always did. "I love you, sweetheart," he said, and then he took her in his arms and they whirled through the darkened library, passing between the desk and the fireplace, the pool table and the leather sofa where at least one president had sat.

The dance ended when Zachary lifted Kristin off the floor, pressing her body to his even as their mouths met. Their tongues sparred, greedy for conquest, and Kristin gave a little whimper of welcome as she felt one of Zachary's hands curve around her breast.

He set her on the edge of the pool table and nuzzled her neck with warm, moist lips.

Kristin trembled when he gently lowered her bodice, baring both her breasts. They glowed like alabaster, tipped with rose, and stood out proudly for Zachary's caress.

"I missed you so much," she managed.

He kissed her again, thumbs moving over her nipples, fingers supporting the sweet, plump weight of her. Finally he broke away. "God kelp me, Kristin," he rasped, "I need you—I want you—"

Kristin laid her palms to either side of his face and pressed him to her breast, where he took suckle at a waiting nipple. With his hand he sought a pathway through the voluminous billows of Kristin's skirts.

He circled her nipple with the tip of his tongue before raising his head and chuckling. "Darlin', I need a little aiding and abetting here. I can't find you under all this lace and satin."

Kristin's laugh caught in her throat as she felt his lips close over the pulsing tip of her breast again. She moaned as he pressed her back onto the cool felt of the pool table, and the motions of her fingers were nothing short of frantic as she raised her skirts for him.

"Yes," he whispered, bending to nip her lightly through her panty hose.

Kristin's breath was quick and shallow. Delicious tension coiled within her as Zachary gently rolled down her hose and tossed them aside. She gasped when he brought her heels up to rest on the edge of the pool table.

"I'm going to enjoy this a great deal, princess," he told her, his lips moving against the satiny flesh of her inner thigh. "And so are you."

Kristin's first release came rapidly; it rumbled deep within her, like an earthquake, and left her shuddering in a series of mellow aftershocks.

"We're going to have to do better than that," Zachary said, as he proceeded to bring her to the brink of an emotional volcano. "Much better."

"Just take me," Kristin pleaded softly as he consumed her. "Please, Zachary—"

He lifted his head. "I'm only giving in because I'm so damn desperate," he replied. In the next moment he was inside her, and Kristin was buoyed up on geysers of hot lava. She was a sacrifice. Her flesh was molten, she became a part of the liquid rock flowing from the center of the earth.

And Zachary swallowed her cries of passion even as he sent his own hurtling into her throat....

Kristin came out of her reverie and was disgruntled to find tears on her cheeks. She wiped them away with dusty palms and looked around.

There was no sign of Zachary, and everything was quiet. Too quiet.

She went to Zachary's pack and rifled through it, just in case he might have another candy bar tucked away in there somewhere. Sure enough, there was one, mashed to bits but made of chocolate nevertheless. And he was hiding a well-thumbed paperback mystery as well.

Since she hadn't read anything since she'd left the palace, Kristin was as hungry for the book as she was for the candy bar. She opened them both, and gobbled them simultaneously.

Of course, the chocolate was gone first. She was up to page seventy-four in the book when she thought she heard the nicker of a horse.

Jubilation surged within her, followed immediately by fear. The rebels definitely had horses and Jascha's patrols would, too. Someone was approaching, but it wasn't necessarily Zachary.

Wildly, Kristin looked around for shelter. There was nothing except for a shallow recession in the hillside, where the shadows might hide her.

She dragged both backpacks over to it and hid them, along with herself. Her knee gave silent screams of pain at the sudden exertion, and her heart thumped against her breastbone in fright. She watched with wide eyes, her breath solid as a peach pit in her throat as the sounds grew nearer.

And then Zachary rode into sight, looking none the worse for wear and leading Kristin's horse behind his.

"You did it!" she cried, scrambling out of the indentation, ignoring the agony in her knee and brushing away the cobwebs that clung to her hair. "You got the horses back!"

Zachary grinned wearily as he dismounted.

"What did you do?" Kristin demanded eagerly. In spite of the fear she felt, she was caught up in the drama of imagining the scene. Zachary must have been magnificent.

"I gave them money."

Kristin was momentarily deflated, but she was too glad to see the horses—and Zachary—to dwell on the fact that things hadn't gone as they would have in an adventure movie. She went to the mare she'd come to think of as her own and patted its neck affectionately.

"We'd better get moving while there's still some daylight left," Zachary said, and Kristin realized that he was watching her with a peculiar expression in his eyes.

"Is something wrong?"

He shook his head. "Where are the packs?"

"In there," Kristin answered, pointing toward the cave that wasn't a cave. "I wasn't sure it was you when I heard the horses, so I hid."

Zachary nodded and went to retrieve the packs. He found the mystery, too, with page seventy-four dog-eared. "You know I hate it when people do this to my books," he grumbled, holding the volume up as damning evidence. A moment later he carefully closed the book and tucked it into the pocket of his jacket.

Before Kristin could apologize and point out that she still had a hundred and fifty pages of the story to read, Zachary stormed over to her with his hands on his hips.

It was his standard intimidation pose, and Kristin didn't intend to be swayed by it.

"Come to think of it," he began, "what were you doing going through my pack?"

"I was looking for a candy bar," Kristin responded, folding her arms. "And I found one. You lied to me, Zachary—you said you didn't have any more!"

With a muttered curse he turned away from her, grasped her pack and practically flung it onto her back. "Since you won't be walking, you can carry this," he said as he fastened it.

Kristin glared at him, but it wasn't anger that soured her expression. It was pain. "You're doing it again," she accused.

He practically hurled her up onto her horse's back. "Doing what?" he snapped.

"Making a distance between us. Refusing to talk about what you're feeling. We're mad at each other! Why can't we just fight, like other people?"

The brim of Zachary's hat hid his face. "We have nothing to fight about," he muttered. And then he turned away.

"The hell we don't!" Kristin yelled, making her horse dance nervously beneath her. She watched with grim satisfaction as Zachary's shoulders stiffened under the worn, supple leather of his jacket. "I walked out on you. Didn't that make you angry?"

He turned and, for just a moment, Kristin was frightened by the raw emotion she saw in his face. Then, typically, he regained the formidable control that had probably served him well as an agent. "I wasn't surprised," he answered in an even voice. "I knew you'd feel the pea under our mattress, like a real princess, and go looking for a softer bed."

If Kristin had been close enough, she would have slapped him with all her might. "You bastard, are you insinuating that I left because I cared for someone else?"

His shoulders moved in an insolent shrug. "A princess needs a prince," he replied coldly, and then he turned and mounted his horse.

Kristin felt as though he'd backhanded her. She was torn between conflicting needs to cry and to rave like a wild woman, but she did neither. She just rode along behind Zachary, her teeth sunk into her lower lip, wishing she'd never come back to Cabriz at all.

They rode for hours before they stopped in a densely forested place that sheltered the mouth of a cave.

Kristin got down from the horse before Zachary could help her, biting back a cry at the response of the muscles in her knee, and began unbuckling her pack. She'd had to go to the bathroom for a long time, but she'd suffered in silence, too proud to ask Zachary for a break.

He was making up time, undoubtedly anxious to get her into Rhaos and off his hands.

Kristin went into the woods, attended to her business and returned. "There's a stream back there," she said in tones she might use to address a stranger. "I washed my hands in it."

Zachary had unsaddled the horses and tied them to separate stakes. "Fine," he said.

It was probably her exhaustion, Kristin told herself, and her injured knee, that brought tears so close to the surface. "Are we going to have a fire?" she asked, and her voice trembled. Zachary might be unpleasant, but having him ignore her was like being alone in that vast wilderness.

He nodded and disappeared into the timber without another word.

Kristin found a stump and sat down on it, despondent and bone tired. If she survived this ordeal and made it back to the United States, she vowed she would burrow in somewhere and write one hell of a book about the experience.

Of course, she'd leave out the times Zachary had made love to her. Those memories were naturally too private to share with the world. And too precious.

Zachary returned to camp with an armload of wood, which he tossed down in front of the cave. He glanced at Kristin once or twice as he laid the fire, but he was too damn stubborn to say anything. And that left Kristin with no choice.

"I'd like to finish that mystery novel, if you don't mind," she said.

He pulled it from his pocket and with a flick of his wrist sent it winging toward her.

It landed close enough that she could pick it up without leaving the stump. "Thank you."

Zachary crossed his stomach with one arm and bowed deeply, and there was no humor in the gesture, only mockery. "At your service, your ladyship."

Kristin bolted off the stump and limped over to him. "Damn you, Zachary, stop patronizing me! All I want is a little honest conversation. Is that too much to ask?"

"Honest?" he rasped, towering over her, wrenching off his hat and flinging it aside. His hair, damp with sweat and crusted with dust, bore the impression of it. "You walked out without even giving me a chance to talk to you! Do you call that honest?"

"So you *are* angry."

"You're damn right I am! I loved you, lady! For six months after you left, I spent most of my time lying on the living-room floor, listening to somebody-done-me-wrong songs! I couldn't eat, I couldn't sleep, I couldn't think!" He leaned forward until his nose was a fraction of an inch from hers. "You, on the other hand, were probably running around with the prince!"

Kristin swallowed. She'd wanted Zachary to vent his anger, but she hadn't guessed how intense it would be. "I wasn't 'running around' with anybody," she said quietly. "Jascha and I were old friends. When he found out I was hurting, he wanted to help."

"You were hurting?" The question was harsh, like the rusty blade of a saw grating against metal. "Why, princess? Were your charge cards at their limits?"

Kristin stood her ground, refusing to be daunted. "I'm getting tired of your snide comments about my life-style and my background, Zachary Harmon! Maybe I've been a little indecisive in the past, but I'm a good person!"

She watched as the muscles in his jawline tensed, then relaxed again. After giving her a look of utter contempt, he turned and started to walk away.

Kristin caught hold of his arm and held on with all her strength. "I'm sorry I hurt you," she said when he glanced back at her.

He wrenched free of her grasp and straightened his jacket with a shrugging motion. "Hurt me? Sweetheart, it would have been kinder if you'd taken a hammer to my knee-caps." With that, he returned to the fire and Kristin hobbled back to the stump, sat down and purposefully opened the mystery novel.

She gave up trying to read it after only one attempt; the print was blurred.

Once the fire was going, Zachary took something from his pack and disappeared into the woods. Kristin watched him vanish over the top of the paperback and dragged herself over to the blaze when he was gone. The heat felt good against her knee.

She was still sitting there, dazed with heartache and plain weariness, when Zachary returned, carrying two large fish on a stick.

Her stomach rumbled at the thought of something fresh to eat, but she was careful to hide her eagerness. "I didn't know you liked to read mysteries," she said, almost defiant in her insistence that they carry on some sort of conversation. Actually, there were a great many things she didn't know about Zachary.

Zachary didn't look at her as she brought a lightweight aluminum frying pan from his pack and set it over the coals. "That's one of my grandfather's," he said, his voice so low that it was barely audible.

Kristin remembered then that Zachary had been raised by his widowed grandfather. She turned the book in her hand and studied the battered cover. "A Dan Harmon mystery," the blurb read. "I guess when you read this you feel close to him," she ventured.

He looked at the book, then at her face. He didn't have to say his grandfather had been the only person in the world to give a damn about him, the belief was plain in his hazel eyes.

"When did he die?" Kristin asked. She couldn't remember Zachary sharing even that.

"The year I graduated from college," Zachary answered somewhat to Kristin's surprise, laying the fish he'd caught in the pan.

She put her hand on his arm; he brushed it off.

"Zachary—"

"Just leave me alone, Kristin," he bit out, rising to his feet again and walking away.

Kristin dropped her eyes to the novel, opened it to the dedication page. "For Zachary," it read. With a sniffle and a squaring of her shoulders, she flipped forward to page seventy-four and began reading.

The fish burned, but Kristin ate her share anyway, along with what was left of Zachary's.

"How's your knee?" he asked finally, as she lay propped on her elbows, reading by the light of the fire.

"It's okay," Kristin lied, turning a page.

"The cousin did it," Zachary announced.

It was a moment before Kristin realized he'd just given away the ending. And she was a mere fifteen pages from the finish.

"He did not!" she cried, slapping him on the shoulder with the book.

"With a monkey wrench," Zachary added.

Kristin looked at the last page. "That was mean-spirited," she protested when she saw that he was right.

He smiled at her, but there was no humor in his face or in his eyes. "Maybe I feel mean," he replied. And then he got up and laid out his sleeping bag beside the fire.

It shouldn't have bothered Kristin that he didn't join their two bags together, but it did. She felt a sting in her heart.

"You're not the first person who's ever had a hard childhood, Zachary," she pointed out reasonably. "Or been hurt when a relationship went wrong."

"All right, Kristin," he invited, his tone cutting straight through her flesh to her soul. "Tell me how tough it was to be the only daughter of an ambassador."

"Will you stop playing Oliver Twist, please? Maybe you didn't have the privileges I did, but your grandfather was not a poor man. And my home life wasn't so great. My father never offered me one scrap of encouragement or respect in my life!''

Zachary said nothing for a long time, but when he did speak, his words left Kristin shaken. ''I called you once. After you left.''

The words stunned Kristin so much that for a long time she could only sit there, trying to absorb them. ''You did?''

''Yes.'' Plainly, he wasn't going to give anything away. She would have to work for every word.

''Where was I?''

''Williamsburg. You were there with your parents and the prince—remember?''

Kristin was filled with an overwhelming sadness, and the beginnings of outrage. No one had told her about Zachary's call. ''I didn't know,'' she said, thinking about her father. *If I survive this, Dad, you and I are going to war.*

''I talked to the ambassador.'' Zachary's voice was calm, matter-of-fact.

Kristin squeezed her eyes shut. ''He didn't tell me.''

Zachary gave a raw, mirthless chuckle. ''The ambassador never saw me as an acceptable son-in-law,'' he replied, surprising Kristin. She'd expected him to accuse her of lying. ''And I'll be damned if he wasn't right. You and I would never have made it, princess. We didn't have anything going for us except great sex.''

Kristin was glad of the darkness; it hid the tears that had brimmed in her eyes at his words. ''You're right,'' she said with all the dignity she could summon. ''We should never have gotten together in the first place.'' She rolled out her sleeping bag, took off her shoes and crawled into bed. She'd wanted to fight it out with Zachary, and she'd gotten her way.

She hadn't counted on losing.

Seven

Kristin's sleep was fitful that night; she missed the warmth and substance of Zachary's body lying next to hers. Several times she awakened and reached for him, only to remember that another rift had opened between them. And this time there would be no crossing the chasm.

Morning brought chilly fog and the welcome smell of something frying. Kristin sat up, drawn out of her sleeping bag by the almost-visible aroma. "Umm?" she muttered, hugging herself. "What is that?"

Zachary spared her a scant smile. "Corned beef mixed with freeze-dried potatoes and powdered eggs," he answered. "It tastes better than it sounds."

Kristin shook her head as he handed her a mug of his special camp-fire coffee. "You really are a marvel. Did they teach you this in secret agent school?"

Again he smiled, but there was something sad in the response that touched Kristin's heart like the back of a cold spoon. "I learned it from my grandfather. He had periodic yearnings to return to the land, like his hero."

"Who was?" Kristin prompted, taking a cautious sip of the hot, delicious coffee.

"Henry David Thoreau," Zachary replied. He wasn't looking at her then; he was busy dishing up his breakfast concoction. "Eat hearty, princess. I have a feeling today's going to be a challenge."

Kristin felt reasonably contented, except for a distinct case of heartbreak, as she accepted the plate he handed her. She thanked him automatically, but her brow was furrowed as she tried to catch his eye. "Why should this day be any worse than the rest?"

"Just a hunch," he answered, his voice low, his eyes scanning the trees that surrounded the cave.

Because she was hungry and the food smelled so good, Kristin began to eat. "You know," she said after swallowing, "if you ever get tired of teaching, you could always work as a short-order cook."

Zachary chuckled at that, albeit reluctantly. He was pulling his familiar trick of distancing himself from her, and he was all too adept at the technique. "Thanks, princess. I'll remember that."

Kristin was lonely for their old bristly camaraderie, and she tried to fan the flames of the conversation. "Do you like teaching?"

He shrugged, chewing. "It's all right," he said presently.

"But it isn't what you really want to do?"

His eyes linked with hers briefly, then turned away. "Sometimes," he said in quiet tones, "a man can get his life so screwed up that nothing pleases him, no matter how good it is." With that cryptic statement, he turned his concentration to his breakfast.

Kristin cleaned her plate, even though there was a lump in her throat, then got out of the sleeping bag to walk down to the stream and clean up. She yearned for a hot bath, clean clothes and a real bed, surrounded by solid walls, in a country with a stable government.

"How's your knee?" Zachary asked when she returned to camp. She'd groomed herself as best she could and washed her plate so it wouldn't appear that she had to be waited on all the time.

"It still hurts a little," Kristin replied honestly. "But I think it's getting better."

He was sipping coffee, and his gaze never quite met hers. "Maybe I'd better examine it."

Kristin's temper flared. "Heaven forbid," she said. "Then you'd actually have to look at me!"

His hazel eyes came swiftly to her face, fiery with some emotion Kristin didn't want to recognize. "Take your jeans off," he ordered brusquely.

In spite of all the times they'd made love, Kristin's cheeks went crimson at the suggestion. "No."

Zachary advanced toward her. "I'm going to look at your knee, Kristin, whether you take your jeans off or I do. The choice is yours."

Now it was Kristin whose gaze was averted. "I'm fine, really."

"Let me see." He was nearer now; she could feel him towering over her.

She knew she'd lost. With her teeth digging into her lip, she undid the snap and zipper of her jeans, pushed them toward her knees and sat down on the tree stump. "If anybody sees us," she said in a voice barely above a whisper, "I'll never forgive you!"

"If anybody sees us," Zachary countered, squatting down on his haunches to lay gentle fingers on her bruised, swollen knee, "we'll both be in big trouble. This is one time when we don't want the cavalry riding to the rescue."

Kristin winced involuntarily as he touched her knee, and he gave her an angry look.

"I'm glad it's better, princess," he said with cold sarcasm, "because if it were any worse, you'd need to be in a hospital."

"It isn't as bad as it looks," Kristin insisted, and when Zachary stood she followed suit, quickly pulling up and refastening her jeans.

He turned and walked away, only to return a few moments later with two pills in his hand. "Here," he said, holding out his palm. "They're just aspirin, but that might help."

"You've got practically everything in that pack of yours," Kristin said, trying to lighten the moment a little. "I don't suppose you have this week's issue of *People*?"

Zachary grinned in spite of himself. "Sorry, princess. The aspirin was it. Swallow them while I saddle the horses."

Kristin returned to the stream and knelt beside it, scooping up the cold, fresh water in her palms after tossing the aspirin into her mouth. An eerie feeling possessed her as she swallowed; it was as though she was being watched.

Shivering, she got awkwardly to her feet and looked around. Seeing nothing, she made her way back to camp.

Zachary helped her into her pack, making her feel a little like a child in a snowsuit with a balky zipper, then hoisted her onto her horse. The day ahead looked long and cold to Kristin, as well as painful, and she didn't have the heart to ask again how long it would be until they were over the border into Rhaos.

She knew she wouldn't like the answer.

They rode uphill throughout the morning, raising a lather on the patient horses, and the aspirin did little to quiet the persistent ache in Kristin's knee. It didn't help that she'd hurt that same joint during a game of tennis the year before, but nothing could have made her complain. She wasn't the spoiled princess Zachary thought she was, and she was going to prove that if she accomplished nothing else beyond survival.

During those first few hours Zachary spoke to her only once. He turned as they were about to pass through a narrow opening between two enormous rocks and said, "You'll be able to see the Rhaotian border in another few minutes."

Kristin was elated, though her joy was tinged with a shading of sadness because she knew she and Zachary would soon be parting forever. She wished, for one wild moment, that she could have conceived Zachary's baby; at least then she wouldn't have lost him entirely.

In the next few seconds it seemed that the world was shifting on it axis. One moment Kristin was lamenting the impossibility of pregnancy, the next she was frozen with horror.

Just as she followed Zachary through the cleft in the rocks, men in shabby trousers and shirts came from every direction, including overhead. They shouted and shrieked, and their faces were twisted with vicious concentration.

Zachary fought, but he was vastly outnumbered. They wrenched him from the saddle and swarmed over him.

Through it all she heard him shout, "Run, princess! Get the hell out of here!"

Kristin couldn't have left even if she'd wanted to. Her muscles were rigid with fear, her eyes wide. Bile rushed up into her throat as she watched the men beating Zachary.

Only when he fell unconscious to the ground did she scream.

She was dragged from her horse only moments later, and she had no reason to expect a fate different from Zachary's. She braced herself, but the men only shuffled her along between them, their hands strong on her arms.

She looked back over one shoulder to see Zachary being half propelled and half dragged behind. *Don't hurt him any more,* she pleaded silently. Behind her the horses nickered and whinnied in confusion and panic. Kristin's hands were tied and she was flung unceremoniously into the back of a Jeep.

A bolt in the floor scraped her cheek, and her knee hurt so badly that she thought she might be sick. For all that, her mind and soul were full of Zachary. Where was he? What had they done to him?

Kristin squeezed her eyes shut and offered a silent prayer. *If one of us has to die, God, let it be me. Zachary was only trying to help.*

The Jeep's engine roared to life, and the dusty vehicle began to jolt and jostle its way down the mountainside. Kristin wondered whether their captors were rebels or guerrillas fighting on Jascha's side.

Either way, she and Zachary were in more trouble than the wildest imagination could have dreamed up.

Kristin consoled herself with the idea of writing a book about her experiences—should she be fortunate enough to survive. At the moment it looked as if she was bound to die young.

And probably in intense pain.

After what seemed like hours, the Jeep finally came to a lurching stop. Once again, strong brown hands lifted her, and she nearly fainted at the protest in her knee when the men set her on her feet.

"Who are you?" she asked angrily in her halting Cabrizian, and her captors laughed. There must have been a hundred of them, and there were at least twenty Jeeps.

A group of ramshackle huts stood nearby, their roofs covered with taut animal skins. Curious children and women, in the same trousers and pants as the men, gathered around, staring. Kristin turned her head, searching for Zachary, but there was no sign of him.

Dear God, Kristin thought, her numb hands still bound behind her, maybe they'd already killed him. Left him lying on the ground . . .

Hot tears filled her eyes. *Zachary,* she called silently.

She distinctly heard a response, though the sound seemed to come from inside her own head. *I told you this was going to be a bad day.*

The words were so distinctly Zachary's that Kristin actually smiled. He was alive, then. And he was nearby.

The relief nearly made her sag to the ground; the strangers pulled her roughly back into an upright position.

It was only later, when she'd been thrown onto a pile of skins in one of the huts, her hands still tied tightly behind her back, that she began to analyze the experience and thus to doubt it. She'd only thought she heard Zachary speak to her; she didn't have psychic episodes and neither did he.

Her heart was so heavy that she just lay still for a long time, held down by the weight of her sorrow. If Zachary died because of her silly fantasies about marrying a prince and ruling over a storybook land, she was never going to forgive herself.

Not that she was likely to live much longer than he did.

Finally Kristin struggled into a sitting position and looked around. There was no one else in the hut, although she could hear excited voices outside, arguing in rapid Cabrizian. Although she'd forgotten most of the language, she got the gist of the conversation—one faction was in favor of rape, the other wanted to sell her back to the prince.

She lowered her head. It probably hadn't been difficult to figure out that she was Jascha's runaway bride. She and Zachary were without a doubt the only Caucasians in the entire country. What had made them think they could get away?

Presently a woman came in. She brought a ladle of water and held it to Kristin's lips. Thinking of typhoid and hepatitis and all the other diseases that flourished in these remote villages, Kristin drank. She was simply too thirsty to refuse.

"My friend," she began, grappling with the language. "Is he well?"

The woman, who wore the prescribed trousers and shirt, did not look at Kristin. Nor did she answer. She just scurried out of the hut and let the crude wooden door fall shut behind her.

"Excuse me," Kristin called, lapsing into English in her frustration. "Excuse me, but I need to use the bathroom!"

There was no answer, and Kristin sat in utter misery, her wrists throbbing where the thongs chafed against her skin, her fingers so numb she couldn't feel them. Her heart and her knee, however, fairly pulsed with pain, one keeping time with the other.

After a long time the woman returned and untied Kristin's hands. She chattered incomprehensibly and shook one finger, then led her captive toward the door.

Kristin took the indecipherable discourse as a warning and tried to look submissive as she followed her keeper out into the afternoon sunlight. Another look around reinforced the dismal fact that there would be no escaping.

The woman led her to a pit some distance from the village. Even in the cool, crisp air there were flies, and the stench was enough to curdle Kristin's stomach.

Nonetheless, she did what she had to do and allowed herself to be ushered back to camp.

Again, she searched eagerly for Zachary as she passed among the people. Again, there was no trace of him.

Inside the hut, the woman tied Kristin's hands behind her back again, though this time the thongs were not pulled so tightly. She sank down onto the skins, which were considerably cleaner than the ones she and Zachary had slept on in that other hut just a few nights before, and closed her eyes.

There had to be a way out of this situation, she thought. Perhaps if she told the men her father would pay ransom...

But that would be difficult. Someone would have to bring the money into Cabriz, and a trade would need to be made. There would be nothing to stop her captors from taking the money and still killing her and Zachary, as well as the messenger. Provided a messenger could be found in the first place.

Cabriz wasn't exactly a hot tourist attraction at the moment.

Kristin's reflections were interrupted when the door of the hut opened again and one of the men came in, carrying a rifle across one arm. His eyes were quick, black and mean, and they skittered over Kristin's prone figure like a stone over smooth water.

Instantly she tensed. "Don't touch me," she breathed in English, too frightened to search her mind for the Cabrizian words.

The man laughed and spoke to her in her own language, though his words were so heavily accented that she could barely make them out. "You cannot afford to give orders, pretty one."

Kristin was silent, watching him, waiting.

He squatted beside her, reached out to sift her hair through grubby fingers. She tried to pull away; he tightened his grasp and gave the lock a painful wrench.

"The prince will pay much money for you," he said. "And for your friend."

Kristin tried to suppress the shudder that went through her. Jascha would not be forgiving of her actions or of Zachary's—it was the code of his culture to take vengeance when it was called for. To do anything less would be to lose face. "You are rebels," she said calmly. "Why would you want to please the prince?" She paused, swallowed. "My father is rich. He'll give you more money than Jascha would, if you'll just let us go."

The rebel laughed and thumped his chest with one fist. "You think we are fools? The prince will give us more than gold. He will pay in guns and prisoners, and medicine and food."

Kristin knew he was probably right. And that Jascha would make her and Zachary wish they'd never been born long before he finally relieved them of their lives. "So you're turning us over to the prince?"

Her visitor nodded, black eyes glittering. "Tonight you stay," he said, and once again his gaze ran the length of her.

"You'd better not lay a hand on me," Kristin said, operating on pure bravado as she struggled to sit up. It was an awkward pursuit, with her hands caught together behind her that way. "I was to be the prince's wife. He won't pay if you've used me."

He gestured toward the door with a slight motion of his dark head. "The other one, he use you. And Jascha will kill him for it." A slow, insolent grin spread across the man's face.

Kristin thought it was probably a good thing she was bound; otherwise, she would have slapped him. "Jascha's a jealous man. He'll kill you, too. And all your friends."

The rebel gave a shout of laughter at that. "He try. He fail. I do what I want."

Kristin's blood turned cold in her veins, but she kept her chin high and her gaze remained defiant. Not for one moment did she think her opponent was intimidated; his boast had not been an idle one. He could do what he wanted, and Kristin had no real way to protect herself.

But suddenly an argument erupted outside, just when she thought all was certainly lost, and the man disappeared.

Although she was nearly faint with relief, Kristin couldn't allow herself to fold. She scrambled to her feet and sneaked to the door, pressing her ear to the wood. The rebels were still engaged in their earlier debate, one side in favor of savagery and murder, the other leaning toward the money, food and guns Jascha could provide.

Kristin didn't find either prospect appealing, but of course she would have chosen being returned to Jascha if they'd offered her an option. That, at least, would give her and Zachary some time to escape.

When she heard someone approaching the hut, a man talking in a voice as loud and angry as the others, she drew back, eyes wide, wondering if the prisoners' fate had at last been decided. Whatever happened, Kristin hoped she wouldn't have to see Zachary suffer.

The door opened and a man came in. He was older than the first visitor, and he moved with authority. "Hakan," he said, tapping his chest with one finger. Then he pointed the same digit at Kristin.

"Kristin Meyers," she answered.

He took her arm in a firm but painless grasp and turned her, and Kristin's cheeks burned. He was assessing her value, just as he might that of a brood mare or a ewe in the marketplace.

With a cocked thumb, he gestured toward the door. "Harmon is your man?"

Kristin knew Zachary would love that question, their circumstances notwithstanding, and she vowed he'd never hear about it—or know what her answer had been. "Yes," she said with a lift of her chin. There was always the chance the men in the village wouldn't trouble her if they thought she belonged to someone else. Even among bandits there was a code where such things were concerned.

Hakan laid the palm and splayed fingers of one hand over Kristin's belly, and while she flinched, she forced herself not to try to wrench away. "Make child?"

She shook her head. "No. I—I can't make children." She wasn't about to explain why; it was none of Hakan's business.

The shrewd leader looked surprised, then downright contemptuous. "No make child, what use?" he asked.

Kristin's responses were necessarily limited. This guy wouldn't care that she could put on a party for two hundred people or write a sparkling article for the social pages of a magazine or newspaper. Nor would it matter that she played a mean game of tennis.

To his way of thinking, and that of the rest of his culture, women were good for two things—cooking and making babies.

"I can cook," she lied.

Hakan's expression revealed frank skepticism. Again, Kristin had the feeling that if Zachary had been there, he would have laughed. "You go Jascha," he decided. "We take money. Guns."

For all that she'd just been given a reprieve of sorts, Kristin was vaguely insulted. She held on to her temper, reminding herself that this was no time to indulge in tantrums. "What about my friend?"

Hakan smiled, revealing large yellow teeth. "Jascha pay much for him. More for him than for you."

"Could I see him, please? My friend?"

Hakan's lip came down like an automatic garage door, and the smile disappeared. "No!" he raged. And for a moment Kristin thought he was going to strike her.

Although her every instinct called for it, she refused to cower. "He won't be any use to Jascha if he's hurt," she reminded Hakan in a reasonable tone of voice as he turned away to open the door. "Please. I want to see him."

The man turned and studied her for a long moment, and she thought she saw something like respect flicker in his eyes. Whatever the emotion was, it was gone in the space of a heartbeat.

"Come," he said tersely. "You see Harmon."

Silently thanking a friendly fate, Kristin stepped toward the door. Hakan took her arm and thrust her outside, into the last blazing brightness of the sun. In just a few hours it would be dark.

While the other rebels looked on in silence, Hakan led Kristin across the village to another hut, opened the door and gestured.

Because she'd just come from darkness into blazing light and was now going into gloom again, Kristin had to pause a moment on the threshold to let her eyes adjust. When they had, she saw Zachary lying half-conscious on the floor.

Kristin turned her head and looked Hakan straight in the eye. "Untie my hands," she ordered.

The rebel leader paused a moment, probably stunned by her audacity. Then, remarkably, he reached down and loosened the thongs binding her wrists together. His face left no doubt in her mind that his leniency had distinct limits. "You try to run away, we kill," he said.

Kristin nodded and turned toward the only man she'd ever loved. "I need cold, clean water and some cloth," she said to Hakan. And then she went and knelt beside the prone form on the dirt floor of the hut. "Zachary?"

His hand locked around hers. "Princess." He breathed the word, rather than speaking it. His eyes didn't seem to focus, and his face was covered with dried blood. "Did they hurt you?"

Although Kristin wanted very much to cry, she knew it would be the worst thing she could do. She kissed his forehead. "Looks like you got the worst of it," she replied gently. "Are any of your bones broken?"

Zachary thought for a moment, then shook his head. "No. But they probably will be soon. When we get to the palace, princess, tell Jascha I kidnapped you—"

Kristin felt her throat tighten. "No. That would only make it worse for you."

"It's going to be bad for me any way you look at it, Kris." His fingers entangled themselves gently in her hair, his thumb soothed her pulsing temple. "There's no reason for you to suffer if you can avoid it. And if you can save Jascha's pride, you'll also save that shapely little rear end of yours."

She wrapped her arms around him, held him close. "Oh, Zachary, I'm so sorry for getting you into this. I was such an idiot, believing in fairy tales—"

The door creaked open, and a woman came in with a basin of water and a piece of cloth. By the time she and Zachary were alone again, Kristin had gathered her frail composure.

Gently she began to wash the blood from his face, too stricken by the cost of her foolishness to talk.

Zachary laid a very dirty hand to her cheek. "Princess, I can handle anything but seeing you hurt. Now promise me you'll mollify Jascha in any way you can."

Kristin ran her tongue over dry lips and shook her head. "No. I couldn't live with myself—"

Zachary's voice was suddenly harsh. "Listen to me. You won't live at all if you don't tell Jascha that I forced you to leave the palace. You think you know the man, but *I* know the culture, and the prince's honor won't be worth spit if he doesn't avenge this."

She let her forehead rest against his. "Okay, Zachary," she said, wanting only to calm him. But even then she knew she couldn't betray him to protect herself. "Okay." She kissed his forehead. "Whatever you say."

He smiled and kissed her lightly on the lips. "Of course, if we get a chance to skip out, we'll take it," he whispered. "Be ready, princess."

Kristin nodded as Hakan came in and pulled her roughly back to her feet. He tied her hands behind her back again, as much for Zachary's benefit, she thought, as his own, and then pushed her toward the door.

There were so many things Kristin wanted to say that she didn't manage to voice one of them. She just looked at Zachary for a long moment, then allowed Hakan to drag her out into the hot sunshine again.

She was taken back to the other hut and, when the same woman returned to keep an eye on her, her wrists were unbound. She was allowed to wash her hands and face in cold water and given a small dish of rice and a bowl-like cup of tea.

Since there were no chopsticks, or utensils of any kind, Kristin ate with her fingers. She was hungry, despite everything, and if the chance to escape presented itself she didn't want to be in a weakened state.

Her knee was hurting again, now that Zachary's aspirin had worn off, but Kristin had other things to think about.

Perhaps, she reflected as she drank the strong, flavorful tea, she could reason with Jascha. Cultural dictates aside, he was a gentle, sensible man. He'd attended college in the United States and, of course, he'd dressed like an American then, though now he seemed to be embracing Cabrizian ways again. Surely Kristin could make him see that a marriage between the two of them would have been a mistake anyway, and that there was nothing all to be gained by punishing Zachary.

By the time Kristin huddled up on the skins to sleep that night, she'd convinced herself that Jascha would forgive her and Zachary both, and let them go back home in peace. Believing that was the only way she could have gotten any rest.

When she awakened to a chilly morning, however, all her doubts returned to haunt her.

Once, she'd truly believed that she knew Jascha. She would have put her very life in his hands. Now, however, logic told her that Zachary was right. The prince had been conditioned by centuries of tradition, and one socialite probably wasn't going to change his mind.

Kristin was given more rice and tea, but this time she couldn't eat or drink. She could think only about all the horrors that might well lie ahead.

It was about ten o'clock, she judged, when she saw Zachary being led from his hut. Like her, he was bound, but his manner was inexplicably cocky. He caught her eye and grinned.

She glowered at him, silently reminding him that he might at least have the good sense to be scared, and his grin stretched from one side of his dirty, bruised face to the other, showing his strong white teeth.

I love you, Kristin thought desperately as she was lifted into the back of another Jeep. *And isn't this a hell of a time to think of it.*

Eight

————

Another rusty bolt bruised Kristin's cheek as she bumped along in the back of the rebel Jeep toward almost certain doom. The bright sunlight was frying her, her head and injured knee were both throbbing and her stomach was threatening revolt, but her mind was on Zachary, not herself.

He wanted to take the blame for what had happened, to spare her from Jascha's rage. She wondered if Zachary knew he still loved her, or if it was a secret his subconscious mind was keeping from the rest of his brain.

Despite everything, Kristin smiled. Zachary loved her. Maybe, if by some miracle they got out of this fix, there was a chance of making their relationship work.

Because present reality was so painful, Kristin let her mind wander into a rosy future, where she and Zachary were married. In her fantasy they were furnishing a large split-level house with a view of the ocean. Zachary was teaching, and she was pregnant and hard at work on the book about Cabriz....

Cabriz. Kristin was jolted back to the floor of that filthy Jeep just as it came to a screeching halt.

What now, she wondered, biting her lower lip. They couldn't have reached Kiri so fast—that would take hours more. She waited, fighting down a wave of panic, until someone came and lifted her out of the vehicle.

She looked around, dazed. There were only two Jeeps now, instead of twenty or more, and Zachary was hand-cuffed to the roll bar of the other one.

Only then did Kristin realize that the rebels couldn't just drive boldly up to the palace door with their prisoners, no matter how valuable. She and Zachary would be hidden until a deal had been struck, and that could take days.

She was both relieved and fearful. The more time that passed before the two of them were turned over to Jascha, the better the chances of their escaping. On the other hand, the rebels could get bored and decide to play a few games of their own.

The driver of the Jeep Kristin had been riding in jabbed her in the back with the tip of a rifle barrel and ordered her to move. She stumbled into the woods toward a hut and prayed that her captor loved his wife.

The doorway was covered only by the tanned hide of some animal, and this curtain was pushed aside as Kristin approached. A tiny Cabrizian man smiled at her, showing broad gaps between his teeth, and gestured for her to come in.

She risked a backward glance and saw that Zachary was behind her. He gave her an almost imperceptible nod, and she stepped into the darkened hut.

Something made with cabbage was cooking on a little oil-powered stove in the corner, but there was no other furniture except for the inevitable pile of skins where the residents probably slept.

To Kristin's surprise, her hands were untied, and she was given water in a cup made of some smoothly polished wood. With trembling fingers—only a little sensation had returned—Kristin held the cup to Zachary's lips.

He resisted for a moment, then sipped. His face and hair were filthy, and every visible inch of his skin seemed to be covered with abrasions, bruises and cuts. Kristin knew he was in pain, but he was too stubborn and too proud to complain.

Although the apparent owner of the house had slipped out, one of the two rebel soldiers who had escorted Kristin and Zachary into the hut was still in evidence. He lost patience and, with a muffled exclamation, slapped the cup from Kristin's hand.

Flames of fury licked to life inside her, and Zachary must have seen their reflections in her eyes.

"Hold your tongue, princess," he said evenly, just as she was about to tell her captor what she thought of his manners. "This guy's not an insolent waiter biding time until he gets his big break in the theater. He's a trained killer."

Kristin averted her eyes and hugged herself, fighting down a rage that was born more of fear and panic than anger.

Since his hands were bound and there was a gun trained on his head, Zachary could offer comfort only by words and the timbre of his voice. "We've got to stay calm, Kris. It's our only chance."

At this the guard grew angry and shouted at Zachary in such rapid dialect that Kristin failed to understand it.

"He wants me to go outside," Zachary explained with a philosophical sigh as he turned toward the door. "Remember, princess—don't needle these bozos. They're all about five seconds from lift-off as it is."

Kristin swallowed. "I'll be careful," she promised.

And Zachary was led out, but she was alone for only a moment. When her guard returned, he handcuffed her to a rusted metal ring lodged in the dirt floor of the hut, restricting her movements so that she could only lie on the smelly skins. She watched him with wide, fearful eyes—his thoughts were plainly visible in his face.

He was wondering if he could get away with raping her.

He must have decided not to risk angering his superiors, because he left the hut, shoving the hide curtain aside with a furious motion of one hand as he passed.

The small man returned almost immediately, but he didn't frighten Kristin so much as the guard had. He'd smiled at her earlier, and she'd seen no irony or hatred in his face.

He knelt beside the skins and spoke to Kristin with gentle patience. He wanted to know why she'd been limping.

Under the circumstances, kindness was an unexpected weapon, and Kristin had no defense against it. She wept softly and told him about the injury to her knee, knowing all the while that he understood nothing beyond the gesture of laying her hand to the offending joint.

He found a knife somewhere and cut a slit up the leg of Kristin's blue jeans, then laid the fabric aside to look at her knee. He prodded the swollen flesh with a careful finger, then crept away into the shadows.

By that time her knee was hurting so badly that Kristin was afraid she'd faint. When her host returned and held a cup containing some warm liquid to her lips, she raised her head and drank.

Sleep consumed her almost instantly, dragging her down into its black, healing folds and secreting her there.

When she awakened, the pain in her knee had subsided and the smell of boiled cabbage was dense enough to choke her. She sat up and squinted, trying to see through the smoky shadows.

Zachary was sitting with his back to the opposite wall, his knees drawn up, holding a bowl to his mouth with cuffed hands. "Feeling better?"

Although her knee was definitely improved—when she touched it gingerly with her free hand she found that the swelling had gone down—Kristin was far from her best. "Just terrific," she answered. "My hair is matted and probably full of bugs, and my skin is so dirty it's a wonder someone hasn't written 'wash me' on my forehead. I'm hungry enough to eat anything that won't try to crawl away from me, and one of my wrists is chained to an iron ring. All in all, Zachary, I'd say 'better' isn't the way I feel."

The thin moonlight seeping into the hut through various cracks and crevices showed that he was grinning. "You're bitching. With you, that's a good sign."

Kristin sighed. "What's in that bowl?"

"Some kind of cabbage and fish concoction. Want some?"

"Every part of me except my stomach is voting no," Kristin answered, brushing tangled hair back from her face.

Zachary chuckled then called out in Cabrizian, and the little man came in. He beamed at Kristin, went to the small, smoky stove, and dished up some soup.

The stuff looked, smelled and tasted terrible, and yet Kristin could hardly keep herself from gobbling it down the way a hungry dog would.

"How do I tell him I have to go to the bathroom?" she asked, once the hunger pangs had stopped gnawing at her middle. Since her host was still smiling at her, she smiled back.

Zachary spoke the dialect deftly, but his request made Kristin lower her eyes and blush a little all the same.

Their gentle guard went out and returned moments later with a rusted tin can.

Kristin looked at it in horror. "He doesn't mean—?"

"He's got orders not to release us under any circumstances," Zachary put in helpfully.

Looking at him more closely, she saw that his feet were hobbled with rope, as well as tied to the same iron ring that held her virtually immobile. "But I need privacy," she sputtered.

"I need a steak dinner, a hot bath and a back rub," Zachary answered. "We're even, princess."

"Hardly," Kristin snapped back, her earlier charitable thoughts fleeing as she considered her predicament.

"This doesn't have to be a problem, your ladyship. I'll turn my head," Zachary offered reasonably, "and Ward Cleaver here will step outside."

Kristin looked in desperation from one male face to the other and finally nodded her capitulation. Her choices were, after all, limited.

"What about those goons with the guns?" she asked, once she'd taken care of the humiliating business and her birdlike host had carried away the can. "Are they around somewhere?"

Zachary shook his head. "They've been gone for hours. It isn't likely they'd want to be in this neck of the woods when Jascha's soldiers come to pick up the spoils of battle."

Kristin had to work up her courage to ask, since she was so afraid of the answer. "When do you think that will be?"

He shrugged. "My guess would be dawn, since both sides are probably anxious to make a deal. But it could be days, or even weeks, if negotiations hit any kind of snag."

Kristin nodded toward their happy jailer. "This guy seems pretty friendly. Maybe if you talked to him he'd see reason and let us go."

The reply was another shake of the head. "I offered him everything from money to a boxcar load of Hershey bars. Not unlike the rest of us, he prefers to keep his hide."

There wasn't much to say after that. Kristin didn't have the courage to ask Zachary if he still loved her; she was too afraid he'd say no.

After an hour, Kristin was given another cupful of the mysterious herbal tea that had taken away the pain and swelling in her knee. She slept soundly, dreamlessly, until she was roughly awakened.

Someone shook her, spoke to her sharply and wrenched her to her feet before she'd even managed to open her eyes.

She recognized Jascha's favorite lieutenant, a solidly built man called Quang. His face was twisted with cruel satisfaction as he spat an insulting Cabrizian word.

"You'll forgive me, princess," Zachary stated as two of Jascha's soldiers hoisted him to his feet, "if I don't defend your honor."

"Kindly keep your smart remarks to yourself," Kristin told him, rubbing the wrist of the hand that had been cuffed to the ring throughout the night.

Quang interrupted the process to manacle her to his own wrist and stride out the door. Zachary, still hobbled and bound, was dragged behind.

The sun was rising, and birds chirped in the trees.

During the ride into Kiri—more Jeeps—Kristin was at least allowed to sit in the front seat with the driver, instead of lying in back on the floor. Her fear increased with every passing mile, and when the palace came into sight she thought her heart would stop beating.

Cruelly, on the way the little procession passed the compound that had once housed the American embassy. The unexpected reminder of long-ago, carefree times nearly brought tears to Kristin's eyes.

Just as they approached the palace, and the towering iron gates swept inward to admit them, a roar filled the sky and the treetops swayed as if caught in a gale. Kristin looked up to see a helicopter hovering over the courtyard.

Jascha.

Kristin suppressed a shudder and lifted her chin a little higher. No matter what happened, she would maintain her dignity.

The Jeep screeched to a stop on the cobblestones in front of a side door. Quang got out of the Jeep, forcing Kristin to climb between the steering wheel and the seat to follow, since she was handcuffed to him.

Inside the palace, in a cool, shadowy entryway, Quang unlocked the cuffs and released Kristin into the custody of Mai and a half-dozen women in robes and veils.

Color climbed her cheeks as they took her arms; these were Jascha's wives—the women who had drugged her the night of the escape with Zachary.

Kristin was filled with fear. She turned wildly in an effort to find Zachary.

His hazel eyes were calm, if weary, as he looked back at her. And his solemn expression reminded her to keep her composure at all costs.

Drawing in a deep breath, Kristin absorbed the courage he lent her and allowed herself to be taken away.

The wives led her upstairs, into Jascha's private living quarters, where they clucked and fussed over her as though she were a naughty child caught playing in a mud puddle in her Sunday dress.

Kristin tried to shift her mind to another place, a secret hideaway in the center of her soul, and made no protest as the women removed her clothes.

A bath filled with hot, scented water was waiting. Under any other circumstances, it would have been pure luxury. Knowing what could lie ahead, it was an ordeal instead.

Kristin was bathed—the women allowed her to shave her own legs and underarms, at least—and her hair was shampooed. The tub was drained and then filled again, and she lay in the fresh water still concentrating on nothing. She couldn't afford to think or feel.

There was a clapping sound, a muttered order, and the wives disappeared like a flock of colorful birds.

Kristin held her breath as Jascha walked into the bathroom.

He wore a tailored navy blue suit with a striped shirt and a smart tie, and his dark hair was expertly cut. He might have been a successful businessman, rather than the future head of the faltering Cabrizian government. Certainly no one expected Jascha's father to return from exile and rule again.

"Hello, Kristin," the prince said, coming to sit on the wide edge of the enormous marble tub.

His brown eyes moved over her naked body, which was only veiled by the water of her bath, not hidden.

She swallowed. Here was her chance. She could tell Jascha that Zachary had taken her away by force and, perhaps, save herself from the prince's vengeance....

"What happened?" Jascha asked reasonably, reaching for one of the enormous white towels Kristin had found so to her liking when she'd first arrived at the palace.

She took the towel and got shakily to her feet, hiding behind the terry cloth as best she could. "I told you before," she said evenly. "I changed my mind. I don't want to be your wife."

Jascha's eyes were hot as he watched her cover herself, even though his manner was still strangely placid. "You love this Zachary Harmon, then—the American who took you away?"

Kristin hesitated. To say she loved Zachary, even though it was the truest thing about her, would only intensify Jascha's yen for revenge. "No," she said. "I only used him. There is a man at home."

"You lie," Jascha accused, and Kristin could see that he was seething. Any moment now he would erupt.

"What are you going to do?" she asked with a tranquillity that surprised even her.

A bitter smile curved Jascha's sculptured lips, and it occurred to Kristin that the situation in his country might have driven the prince a little mad. She had never seen that particular expression on his face before, in all the years she'd known him.

"Jascha?" she prompted, standing on the other side of the vast marble tub, one hand holding the towel tight.

"You will be punished," he said with a sort of pleasant resignation. "And then you will be my wife, as we planned."

Kristin trembled with the effort to raise her next question nonchalantly. "And Zachary?"

Jascha smiled again, as though he anticipated some festival or longed-for gift. "He will die. That, my pretty bride, will be the fate of all your lovers, so I would advise you not to take more."

For a moment, the air around Kristin seemed as heavy and dense as water. There was a queer buzzing in her ears, and she thought she would faint. She swayed, caught herself. "You mustn't do this, Jascha. It's murder. Give me whatever punishment you wish, but don't kill Zachary. *Please* don't kill him.''

"So," Jascha said, and his smile turned sad, philosophical. "You would beg for him. And yet you say you do not love this man."

Kristin drew a deep breath, let it out slowly. "I would beg for anyone, Jascha. It isn't right, taking an innocent life—"

"Innocent?" Jascha gave a bitter chuckle after uttering the word. "Do not think me a fool, Kristin. I felt the fire burning between you and Harmon. I heard your cries in the night as he made love to you."

The color drained from Kristin's face, and Jascha laughed at her shock.

"So it's true," Jascha said with a sort of wounded mockery. He sighed and rubbed his eyes with a thumb and forefinger. "You grieve me, Kristin. I trusted you. I believed you when you said you loved me."

Kristin edged closer to the wall, more afraid and more vulnerable than she'd ever been in her life. "I believed it, too, Jascha—when I said it."

"And now?"

"Now I want to go home."

"This," Jascha said, with aggrieved patience, "is your home." He cocked his thumb toward the sumptuous quarters beyond the bathroom archway. "And that is your bed. You will lie in it whenever I summon you, and you will be a loving wife."

Kristin's hand tightened on the towel, and she tried to sink into the wall behind her.

"Remove that," Jascha ordered, gesturing toward the towel.

Kristin swallowed hard. "Jascha, please..."

"Remove the towel!" he shouted.

Closing her eyes tightly, Kristin forced her fingers to release the fold of terry cloth she held, and she felt cold air touch her flesh as she let it fall.

She sensed Jascha's approach, used all the strength at her command to keep from screaming. His gaze seemed to burn into her skin.

And then his finger curved under her chin. "Open your eyes, Kristin," he said with a deceptive softness.

She obeyed, having no other choice, and her soul went cold at the fury she saw in his face.

"You are very beautiful," he told her, "for a whore."

Kristin stood still, waiting, knowing she had no option but to endure.

Jascha reached down, picked up the towel and draped it almost gently around her. "You will be taken to the room you occupied before," he said. "Dress as you please, but wait there until I send someone for you."

Too grateful for a reprieve, however temporary, to argue, Kristin nodded and proceeded into the bedroom beyond. A blue silk robe had been laid out for her, and she put it on, letting the towel fall away beneath as she closed it, never once meeting Jascha's gaze.

When she bent to pick up the discarded towel, he stopped her. "Leave it," he said, and she did.

He escorted her down the hall to the guest room where she had stayed until the day of her escape with Zachary, and even opened the door for her.

Mai was waiting inside. She'd brought a tray containing hot tea in a delicate porcelain pot, the sugary little cakes Kristin loved and a bowl of fresh fruit.

Jascha went out without a word to either Kristin or Mai.

Kristin ate hungrily, then fondly touched her camera, her journal, the clothes that filled the drawers and the closet. As terrible as her situation was, there was some comfort in having her own things around her again.

When Mai had taken the tray away—and locked the door behind her—Kristin took off the robe and put on clean underwear, a pair of trim gray slacks and a silk shirt in dark blue. Then she sprayed herself with her favorite cologne, brushed her hair and wound it into a French braid, and put on makeup.

After that she paced, waiting, feeling as Anne Boleyn must have felt locked away in the Tower. One hour passed, and then another, and no one came for her.

She got out her journal and wrote, her pen flying rapidly over the pages as she put down memory after memory of her flight with Zachary. And only after the condensed account was completed did she realize that committing what had happened to black and white was probably not the smartest thing she'd ever done.

Anxiously, Kristin searched the room for a place to hide the leather-bound book, but there was none where it would really be safe. She glanced at the hearth and considered burning the volume, but everything within her resisted that. She was a writer, and those pages contained firsthand accounts of her experiences.

Finally, she tucked the journal into a flap in her camera case. That would have to do until she could think of something better.

Kristin began to pace again, but odd noises in the courtyard drew her to the window. She looked out to see a handful of Jascha's soldiers erecting a large wooden pole, and a chill went through her as she watched them hoist it into place.

The sound of a key turning in the lock drew her attention, however, and she turned her back on the strange pillar. The possibility that Jascha had sent for her, or come in person, took precedence over all other concerns.

But it was Mai who entered, moving silently in her gossamer blue gown, her face hidden behind the veil.

"Yes?" Kristin couldn't bear the quiet; if she was being summoned to Jascha, she wanted to know it. "Has the prince asked for me?"

Mai looked at Kristin with exotic, unreadable eyes. "No," she said. "He will not send for you tonight."

Kristin felt hope leap within her. "He won't? Why not?"

The woman glanced away. "He is going."

"Going? Where?"

Mai shook her head, and even as she made the motion, the great blades of the helicopter filled the air with noise. Kristin rushed to the window and saw Jascha getting into the cockpit, along with a woman dressed in a flowing green gown.

"That woman," Kristin said, staring out the window. "She's one of Jascha's wives?"

"Yes," Mai answered softly.

"And you?"

"I am also his wife."

Because Mai had attended her since her arrival in Cabriz, Kristin had assumed the woman was a servant. She watched thoughtfully as the helicopter rose into the air and then swung off sideways toward the horizon. Then she turned to look at Mai. "Surely you don't want your husband to have me for a bride, in addition to the others."

Mai simply looked at the floor. It would not be proper for her to express such an opinion.

Impulsively, Kristin grasped Mai's hands in hers and squeezed them. "Please—you must help me. I've got to find my friend, Mr. Harmon, and leave here before Jascha comes back."

Mai lifted her eyes to meet Kristin's, and they were filled with dread. "No! There is no escaping—not for you or for your Mr. Harmon. There is no way I can help you!"

"You must know where they're holding Zachary."

The woman shook her head. "You cannot help him. He will die when Jascha returns, and you will be punished for your treachery."

Kristin raised a hand to her temple, then lowered it again. There was no sense in arguing with Mai; she would never be able to change her mind. She went back to the window. "That big pole out there—what is it for?"

Mai was silent so long that Kristin finally turned to stare at her.

"Mai?"

"I do not know," said Jascha's wife, so quickly and so fiercely that Kristin knew she was lying.

"Tell me!"

But Mai was in retreat. She opened the door, hurried out and turned the key in the lock.

Kristin looked at the pillar again, shivered, and pulled the thin curtains closed over the window.

The room was full of books—Jascha had been so eager to please her when she first returned to Cabriz—and Kristin needed refuge desperately. She went to the shelves, found a volume of Walt Whitman's poetry and stretched out on her bed to read.

At first her worries made it difficult to concentrate, but she persisted, and finally the beautiful words reached out to enfold and shelter her. They carried her far away from Cabriz, and Jascha, and all the problems she couldn't solve.

Mai did not deliver Kristin's dinner that night. It was brought instead by one of the other wives, a younger woman wearing a pink robe.

"What's your name?" Kristin asked quickly when the girl would have hurried out.

"Tala," a soft voice answered from behind the ever-present veil.

Kristin had no doubt that she too would be forced to cover her face and most of her body once she was officially Jascha's wife.

"What do you think of my marrying the prince?" Kristin asked casually, watching the lovely eyes closely as she spoke. She was, at the same time, pouring tea into a cup.

Tala's eyes flashed fire for a moment. "You will wear white," she said, and the statement sounded like an accusation. Kristin couldn't remember whether white symbolized virginity in Cabriz, the way it did in the Western world. In the East it was the color of mourning.

"I would leave—and not marry Jascha—if you would help me."

"Leave?" Tala failed to keep a note of hope from sounding in that one word.

"If you would just do two things—forget the key to this room when you go out, and tell me where to find Mr. Harmon—"

Tala's eyes grew wide and she retreated a step, shaking her head. "Jascha would be angry."

Kristin took her hand and dragged her forcibly to the window, where she pushed aside the curtain. "That pole out there—what is it for?"

Tala looked at her fearfully. "It is a whipping post," she answered. And then she pulled free of Kristin's grasp and rushed out of the room.

Nine

A whipping post.

Kristin's fingers turned white, so tight was her grasp on the window ledge. Horrible images, splashed with crimson, flipped through her mind.

After several minutes, using every ounce of resolution she possessed, Kristin came away from the window and went to the mirror over the vanity table. She was trembling visibly, her eyes were enormous and there was no color at all in her face.

She began to pace, unable to bear standing still, but the harrowing pictures would not leave her mind. Jascha had deliberately ordered the pillar set up in that part of the courtyard so that she would be aware of its presence at every moment. Which meant Zachary was probably being held somewhere on that same side of the palace, too.

Knowing the fate that awaited them was a form of torture in its own right, and Kristin felt sure Jascha would withhold their punishment until their nerves were shattered by waiting.

Helpless rage surged up into her throat like hot acid. "You bastard," she gasped. Turning back to the vanity table, she picked up the photograph Jascha had given her along with a bevy of other engagement presents, and flung it across the room.

It struck the mantel, and the glass in the frame shattered violently, giving Kristin keen, if temporary, satisfaction.

Zachary hadn't been surprised to find out the palace had a dungeon; he would have bet on it. The bars on his small, dank cell were ancient, like the ones on the single window that looked out onto the courtyard, but they were sturdy.

God knew, he'd tried them often enough.

He looked around at his quarters with a sigh. The furniture consisted of a toilet stained with rust and a metal cot with a thin, filthy mattress.

Because he needed the fresh air, he went to the narrow window and looked out. He could plainly see the pillar—knowing it was there, awaiting him, was part of Jascha's vengeance, of course. What really angered Zachary was the awareness that Kristin could see it, too. And she was probably climbing the walls.

Zachary wasn't a religious man, yet in that moment he prayed devoutly that Hakan, the rebel leader, would go along with the plan he'd suggested. After all, Hakan had people on the inside of the palace, and the chance to double-cross Jascha had to appeal to him in a big way.

With a sigh, Zachary shoved splayed fingers through his dust-encrusted hair and turned his thoughts to his beach house in faraway Silver Shores, his quiet job at the college, his tomato plants. "I'm getting too old for this stuff," he muttered just as a distant clanking sound came to his ears.

Two of Jascha's men appeared in front of the cell, their faces grim. One carried a tray of food, the other pointed a rifle at Zachary, to make sure he didn't try to escape when the door was opened.

"Do I get a last wish?" he asked in leisurely Cabrizian.

The guard set his tray on the bed and backed out of the cell again, never once taking his eyes off Zachary. He didn't answer until the door was safely shut and locked.

"What do you want?"

"A bath," Zachary replied idly, sitting down on the bed and resting the tray across his knees. The conditions in the dungeon were horrific, but the food looked good. "And clean clothes. Jascha's stuff would probably fit."

The guards looked at him in amazement. "You ask to wear the prince's clothes?" one of them marveled.

Zachary shrugged, chewing on a piece of fresh, doughy bread. "Just an idea," he said.

The sentinels went away, muttering between themselves, and Zachary grinned. It never hurt to ask.

He finished the food and shoved the tray through a three-inch gap under the cell door. A rat the size of a full-grown Pekinese immediately appeared to nibble at the leftovers. Zachary wondered if anyone had ever taught a rodent to fetch sticks or roll over and play dead.

He stretched out on the skimpy mattress, his hands cupped behind his head, and watched as the rat finished his meal, gave Zachary a curious inspection and disappeared into the darkness that loomed around the cell like fog.

"So long, Rover," Zachary said with a sigh, closing his eyes.

Immediately he saw a collage of bittersweet portraits—Kristin standing by their bed long ago, wearing one of his shirts and nothing else, holding out her arms to him. Serving him a dinner she'd botched with a sort of forlorn hope in her eyes. Bucking beneath him as they lay in the double sleeping bag on the mountain, their bodies fused.

Pure anguish twisted in his gut. She was going to suffer, unless Hakan came through, and there was nothing he could do to help her. That knowledge was the worst torture of all.

He got up, tried the bars in the window again, found them as immovable as ever. Even if he could have pulled them out, however, he wouldn't have been able to squeeze through the opening.

Hours had passed, the sun had gone down and come up again, before Jascha appeared outside his cell.

"Did you have her?" the prince asked bluntly.

A new energy surged inside Zachary. Even sparring with this bastard was better than pacing or lying on the cot staring up at the ceiling. At least it was something to do. "Yes," he replied.

Although Jascha tried to hide the fact, that single word quivered in its mark like an arrow still vibrating in a bull's-eye. "And she responded to you?"

Zachary shrugged and shoved his hands palms out into the hip pockets of his jeans. "I didn't give her a choice."

Again, Jascha's confidence seemed to waver. "You mean you forced her?"

"Yes." Zachary prayed the prince would believe the lie and grant Kristin some kind of clemency.

Jascha's expression was skeptical, but he gave away nothing more of his private emotions. "I understand that you have had the audacity to ask for a bath and a set of clean clothes."

Zachary's gaze was steady, even though inside he was fighting an urge to beg Jascha not to hurt Kristin. The cool, rational side of his mind knew that would be a mistake. He managed to grin. "You know what they say about Yankees. No manners."

A raw chuckle burst from Jascha's throat, and he shook his head in amused incredulity. "You shall have your bath, Mr. Harmon, and the clothes, too. Never let it be said that I forced you to die in a state of such disarray."

Zachary inclined his head slightly but said nothing. Jascha walked away after giving him a look of undisguised hatred, and two sentries came to fetch him before he had time to lapse into boredom again.

He was manacled between them and led out of the cell and up slippery stone steps into a dusty storage area. From there they entered the kitchen—no one so much as glanced in their direction—and stepped into a service elevator that took them to the upper floor.

Zachary was sure Kristin was behind one of the doors they passed, and he ached to find out which one, but he didn't bother to ask. His escorts probably didn't know, anyway.

They took him into a sumptuous guest suite graced with an enormous marble tub. Three soldiers stood at various points around the room, armed with automatic machine guns.

Zachary grinned to think they considered him so dangerous. In a way it was a compliment.

The guards unmanacled themselves from him and left the room, and Zachary started the taps running to fill the tub, then began taking off his clothes.

"Excuse my impatience, fellas," he said to the soldiers, who looked at him with suspicion. It was obvious they didn't understand English.

He climbed naked into the tub and reached for the fresh bar of soap that had been set out, he suspected, for more esteemed guests. "How about this weather, huh?" he went on, lathering one armpit as he spoke. His prattle unnerved the men, and there was no telling what unexpected advantage that might present.

Zachary scrubbed himself clean, taking his sweet time and talking constantly. He covered politics, professional football, and carried on a one-man debate as to whether the queen liked Diana or Fergie better.

He emptied the tub, rinsed it out and refilled it. Then, lounging, with a mirror in one hand and an old-fashioned razor in the other, he shaved away the stubble of a week's beard.

Not once during any of these processes did he allow himself to reflect on the fact that this might well be the last bath he ever took, but the pillar out in the courtyard was lodged in a dark corner of his awareness like a sliver.

He was given clothes to wear—underwear and socks, comfortably worn jeans and a beige Irish cableknit sweater. He whistled softly as he dressed, put on his own scuffed, dusty boots and carefully combed his hair. There was even a toothbrush and paste, which he used with aplomb, humming through the foam.

At last the ritual could be extended no longer. One of the guards barked an order and gestured with his gun, and Zachary sighed. He waited for the manacles to be put back on, but no one made a move to confine him.

He left the guest chamber with one soldier walking ahead and two behind, but his hands and feet were free, and that filled him with a singular, tremulous sort of hope. He and Kristin might just get their chance after all.

Kristin was too distracted to think about clothes that morning when Jascha sent word that he wished to see her in his study. She put on tan corduroy pants, sneakers and a blue sweatshirt with large, white letters on the front that said God Bless the U.S.A. Her hair was brushed back into the customary French braid and she hadn't bothered with makeup, except for a little mascara and some blusher to give her ashen cheeks color.

Her palms were sweating when she was brought before Jascha's desk, and she rubbed them against her thighs. She tried to smile, out of old habit, but her lips wouldn't make the gesture.

Jascha sat back—at one time he would have risen to greet her—and once again Kristin was struck by the fact that he was a stranger. "I can see that you are thoroughly frightened," he remarked cordially, his hands resting on the tufted arms of his chair. If he had any compunction at all about what he was about to do, she could see no sign of it.

Kristin folded her arms, squared her shoulders and lifted her chin. "Isn't that what you wanted? Does it make you feel better to know I'm afraid?"

At that, Jascha shot out of his chair. "Silence!" he shouted, bending toward her and resting the palms of his hands flat on the surface of the desk.

Terrified, but still too proud to fold, Kristin retreated a step.

Jascha drew a deep breath and let it out slowly. "Harmon tells me that he forced you to submit to him. Is that true?"

Kristin's cheeks ached with color. "No," she whispered hoarsely after a long pause.

"You willingly submitted to his—attentions?"

She nodded. "Yes."

"Why did he lie to me?" Jascha asked, and his tone was a mockery of bewilderment. "What did he hope to accomplish?"

Kristin swallowed. "He wanted to spare me punishment," she said quietly. "But I won't allow him to take the whole brunt of your anger."

The prince laid a hand to his heart. "This is all so touchingly romantic. Tell me, would you also suffer in his place, as he apparently would in yours?"

"Yes," Kristin answered without a moment's hesitation.

"And he did not kidnap you?"

"I left willingly."

The muscles in Jascha's handsome face contorted briefly, twisting it into a frightening mask. He cried out the Cabrizian word for guard, and Kristin's jailers reappeared.

She was taken from the room with one gripping each arm, and her heart rose into her throat and hammered there. The inevitable, she knew, could be avoided no longer.

The sunshine was hot and dazzlingly bright, glaring on the brick surface of the courtyard. Jascha's helicopter sat nearby, unmanned, and the wives, dressed in their colorful gowns, stood like a human rainbow behind a first-floor window, looking on.

Kristin assumed they were present in order to learn first-hand the fate of a disobedient bride. Doubtless, the morning's spectacle would nip any thoughts of unwifely rebellion in the proverbial bud.

She stood between her guards, watching in silence as Zachary was brought from the palace. He was clean, and dressed in jeans and a sweater, and he favored her with a brazen grin. For just a merest moment, Kristin's spirits rose.

Then she remembered that she and Zachary were about to become examples.

She looked around again. Besides Jascha, there were just three soldiers present. No doubt many others were watching from the palace windows.

Jascha gave an order Kristin was too dazed to decipher, and Zachary was thrust forward, toward the ominous pillar. He went right on grinning and tossed the prince a cocky salute.

Fool, Kristin thought miserably. *Don't you know he's about to kill you?* Only then did she notice that Jascha was holding a cruel-looking black whip coiled in one hand.

"You will see now," he said close to Kristin's ear, "what becomes of those who tamper with what belongs to me."

Zachary's arms were taken, and he was hurled against the pillar. Kristin's heartbeat pounded in her ears, and everything seemed to be happening in slow motion, as in a bad dream. Just as the guards were about to bind Zachary's hands together so that he could not step away from the pole, the sky seemed to explode with noise.

A huge, battered helicopter loomed overhead, shadowing the sun. There were shrieks of angry terror as a barrage of machine-gun fire peppered the ground.

Kristin saw Jascha dive for shelter while the guards scrambled for their rifles, neatly stacked against the courtyard wall. Zachary made a sound that was half laughter and half a whoop of triumph and ran toward her.

"Come on, princess!" he shouted, grabbing her hand. "Hakan came through—let's get out of here!"

He grabbed a pistol from a wounded guard and held it on the others as he dragged Kristin toward Jascha's grounded helicopter on a dead run. Kristin looked back, saw troops pouring from the palace doors, but their attention was on the air attack, not the escaping prisoners.

The courtyard was alive with gunfire, but all of it seemed to be coming from the sky.

Swallowing a throatful of bile, Kristin followed Zachary's shouted order and jumped into Jascha's aircraft. The very air seemed to vibrate with the exchange going on outside.

Zachary's hands worked the controls with hasty deftness, and Kristin closed her eyes for a moment and held on.

Overhead, the blades caught, then whirled, deafening Kristin. She put her hands over her ears and looked back once more, just in time to see Jascha pointing at them and yelling orders to the soldiers.

"I hope you know how to fly this thing!" she cried, just as the 'copter lifted off the ground and lurched dizzily away. Bullets pinged against the runners and the aircraft shuddered wildly, but it didn't go down.

Zachary grinned, cocky as hell. "Don't worry, princess," he called back. "I'm a quick study when it comes to things like this!"

Realizing that they were clear of the palace and out of range of the guns, Kristin sagged back against the seat and fought down an urge to be violently sick. "Stop showing off, Zachary," she retorted. "I know you flew a helicopter in the air force."

The city of Kiri fell away rapidly beneath them as they streaked north, toward the border. Below was the timbered mountainside where they had lived out an adventure Kristin would never forget.

"Would you mind explaining how that helicopter happened to show up just when we needed it most?"

Zachary's teeth flashed in an obnoxiously confident grin. "While we were being held at the rebel camp, I made a little suggestion to Hakan."

Kristin remembered the guerrilla leader; he hadn't seemed to her like the sort to take unsolicited advice. "Such as what?"

He shrugged. "I just told him how bent out of shape Jascha would be if the rebels not only collected guns and money for us humble prisoners, but stole us back at the last minute, before the prince could save face."

Kristin was nodding, her brow crumpled in a frown. "But how did Hakan know when to strike?"

Zachary was concentrating on the helicopter controls. "He had people on the inside of the palace, Kristin," he said impatiently. "Haven't you ever seen a James Bond movie?"

Rolling her eyes, Kristin pulled her journal out from under her T-shirt, retrieved a pen from the top of the instrument panel and flipped to a fresh page.

"What the hell are you doing?" Zachary yelled conversationally.

"Writing down how we got away, that we're safe, all that."

Zachary looked regretful. "There is one problem we still have to deal with, princess."

Kristin smiled. Their relationship, of course. Well, with love and work, they could make that fly just like a helicopter. "What?" she asked, only because she wanted Zachary to be the one to say they belonged together.

"We don't have enough fuel to make the border."

Kristin's disappointment was profound. "What?"

Zachary was surveying the rugged country below. "The best we can hope for is a chance to steal a Jeep or a couple of horses. We're running on fumes as it is."

Horror welled up in Kristin at the reality of the situation. "Fumes? Oh, great! Now we're probably going to crash fifty yards from the rebel camp or something! Imagine what Jascha would pay for us now!"

"Well, excuse me!" Zachary bellowed, glaring at her. "Next time we're about to be whipped to death in a palace courtyard, I'll be sure to steal a 'copter with a full tank!"

Kristin's arms were folded tightly across her chest; her journal had slipped, forgotten, to the floor. "Just keep your snide comments to yourself," she snapped.

The aircraft's engine began making an alarming sound midway between a sputter and a pop. Kristin sat bolt upright and screamed as the machine zigzagged drunkenly toward the ground, while Zachary concentrated on grappling with the controls.

They came down in a meadow, and the blades hadn't even stopped whirling when Zachary shoved Kristin out the door and scrambled after her. She went back long enough to grab her journal and the pen, and then Zachary caught hold of her hand and dragged her into the woods at a full run.

"What's the big hurry?" she demanded breathlessly when they were well into the timber.

"Don't be an idiot," Zachary retorted. "By now the attack is over and Jascha's called for another 'copter. He'll be on our trail like a hound dog chasing a fat rabbit!"

Kristin wrenched her hand from Zachary's and walked at a slower pace, struggling to keep her respiratory system from overloading. "If Jascha catches us, we'll wish we'd never been born."

"You always were insightful," Zachary breathed.

"Zachary, this is serious!"

"You're right," Zachary answered, still moving so rapidly that Kristin could barely keep up. "But we're overdue for some good luck."

Kristin hadn't caught her breath. "Where are we going?" she asked impatiently.

Zachary looked back at her, and she saw his jaw tighten. "I spotted a village just before we went down. We're going to try talking them out of a couple of horses."

"Suppose they're bandits—or rebels?" Kristin cried, panicking. "Suppose they sell us to Jascha again?"

He stopped and grasped her by the shoulders, breathing hard himself. "Get a grip on yourself," he ordered, and while his voice and his grasp were hard, Kristin saw concern in his eyes. "We've got to keep moving. Jascha's goons are going to spot that 'copter sooner or later, and we'd better not be in the area when they do. Now, have you got anything we can swap with the villagers, like jewelry or something?''

Kristin attributed her involuntary smile to hysteria and reached under the neck of her sweatshirt to pull out a gold chain with two rings dangling from it. One was a four-carat diamond Jascha had given her when they became engaged, and the other sported a gold lion's head with perfect rubies for eyes. ''How about these?''

Zachary cupped the rings in his hand and whistled as he inspected their design, but when his eyes lifted to meet Kristin's she was unsettled by the shadow of pain she saw move briefly in their depths. ''Where did you get these? I mean, I know the prince gave them to you, but you didn't have them when we were trying to get out of the country before.''

Kristin dropped the chain and rings back down inside her shirt, and she shrugged one shoulder. ''I grabbed them before I left my room this morning. I don't really know why.''

He took her arm, just above the elbow, in a grip just short of bruising. ''Let's keep moving.''

''What's the matter with you?'' Kristin wanted to know as she scrambled along beside him, trying to keep up with his long strides. ''And don't say 'nothing,' Zachary Harmon, because I saw that look in your eyes.''

He stopped and wrenched her against his chest, but it was a gesture of anger, not passion. ''It just reminded me of how little we really have in common, that's all,'' he ground out. ''You're a rich princess, and I'm just an ordinary guy. It's been great, Kristin, and I'll get you out of Cabriz, but after that it's over. I'm never going to look back.''

For several moments Kristin reeled inwardly, just as stunned as if he'd slapped her. ''What?'' she managed to squeak. ''But I thought—''

It was as though a veil had dropped down behind his eyes, hiding the soul Kristin had seen on more than one occasion. A bitter smile twisted his lips. "This isn't a movie, princess. Just because we had great sex and got shot at together doesn't mean we can make a life. It would never work."

Kristin started to protest that she loved him and furthermore that she damn well knew he loved her, but her pride stopped her. She just nodded and pulled free of him.

In another half hour they reached the edge of the village Zachary had seen from the sky. The villagers proved to be curious but friendly, and they gladly accepted Kristin's rings and chain in return for two worn-out plow horses, some blankets and a little food.

"We're spending the night here," Zachary told Kristin when the animated negotiations had been completed and the transaction was made.

"Isn't that a risk?" Kristin asked, and she made her voice sound casual even though just looking at Zachary made her want to cry. She'd had such hopes, such dreams—and he wanted to walk away from her the moment they were safe in Rhaos and never think about her again. "You said it yourself. Jascha's probably right behind us."

"There was a lot of damage to the 'copter when we landed," Zachary answered without looking at her. "I'm hoping they'll think it was a crash and we're already dead."

Kristin felt as though that were the case. She was like a ghost, numb and cold, condemned to wander, never caring where.

She sat with Zachary that evening, staring into the fire while he talked with the villagers in their language, and when he led her to the hut they were to share, she didn't resist. She didn't even argue when he enfolded her in his arms, kissed her forehead and fell asleep, still cuddling her close.

Kristin was exhausted, emotionally and physically, and though she slept, her slumber was not restful. She awakened in the depths of the night, aching with a loneliness so profound, so hopeless, that she was sure nothing could assuage it.

It drove her through the barrier of her pride, that need, and she raised herself to her knees and bent to kiss Zachary's mouth softly.

He stirred, searched her body with his hands, found her breasts. Her name came ragged from his lips, and he moved to pull her down beside him on the skins.

"No," she whispered. "This time is mine." She pushed his sweater up, letting the moonlight seeping in through the roof of the hut dapple his chest. She stroked him, running her fingers through the tangled swirls of golden-brown hair, then bent to taste his nipple with the tip of her tongue.

He moaned. "Kris—"

She rose up again, and calmly unfastened his jeans. "Maybe this will be goodbye," she said. "And maybe you'll walk away without looking back, just like you said. But you'll *never* forget me, Zachary—I mean to see to that."

Kristin bent then to nip at his belly, and she smiled when his manhood was there to meet her.

Zachary groaned and arched his back when she touched him with her tongue. His hands entangled themselves frantically in her hair. Soon he was delirious, begging senselessly in a gravel-rough voice, and Kristin showed him no more mercy than he'd ever shown her.

But at what must have been practically the last second, he gripped her shoulders and in one swift move wrestled her beneath him. His mouth covered hers in a consuming, fiery kiss while his hands moved under her sweatshirt to release her breasts from the restraint of her bra.

"You're right," he rasped as he shoved her sweatshirt up and found one of her nipples with his warm, wet mouth. "I'm never going to forget this night. But damn you, you won't either!"

A whimper escaped Kristin as he took her breast, teased her with his lips and tongue. His hands gripped her wrists, pressing her hands wide of her shoulders into the depths of the skins they lay upon. She writhed under his hips, aware of his length and power in every part of her being.

She grew wilder, more desperate as he made his way to her other breast and sampled that. He held her wrists together above her head now, in one hand, while the other unsnapped her jeans and smoothed them away. He was less patient with her panties, however.

"So beautiful . . ." he told her hoarsely, nibbling his way down over her belly. His tongue moved swiftly through the silken jungle to administer sweet menace.

"Take me," she pleaded. "M-make love to me—please—"

She felt the tip of his shaft at her entrance, teasing, gently prodding.

"Zachary," she sobbed, and he cupped his hands under her bottom and drove into her hard.

The friction set them both afire, and Kristin grasped at Zachary's head and dragged him into a kiss as their bodies rose and fell together in an ancient dance of wonder and need. Her moans collided with his, and their tongues mated frantically.

Kristin felt the sky rushing toward her as despair and joy clashed inside her like great, silent cymbals. Her body convulsed wildly, once, twice, three times, and then she was in the eye of the storm.

Zachary stiffened, gave a low warrior's cry and spilled himself into her, and the two of them lay gasping on the skins for a long time. Kristin cuddled close to Zachary, her arms around his waist, her heart already grieving because there would not be a lifetime of nights just like that one.

When he abruptly thrust her onto her back and loomed over her, Kristin was startled. Her eyes widened when she saw the unrestrained fury in his face, the tears shimmering along his lashes.

"Damn you," he grated out, his thumbs digging into her shoulders. "Why did you do it? Why did you abort my baby?"

Ten

_____

Why did you do it? Why did you abort my baby?

The questions demolished Kristin's spirit like a steel wrecker's ball, and with every strike a little more of her crumbled away.

She opened her mouth to answer, but no sound came out. And Zachary's thumbs were like rivets, bolting her shoulders to the floor.

"Why?" Zachary demanded.

Finally Kristin found her voice. "It was a miscarriage," she croaked, her words barely audible. "I—I wanted our baby, Zachary. I wouldn't have gotten rid of it."

He just stared at her for a long time, his lashes glistening, and she watched as hope and suspicion warred in his face. He thrust free of her and turned away. "You're a liar!" he rasped, and even in the thin moonlight Kristin could see his shoulders shuddering as he struggled to regain control of his emotions. "You were scared—you didn't think our relationship was going anywhere...."

Kristin sat up, wrapping her arms around her knees. She was facing the most crucial conflict of her life—the battle for Zachary's trust—and she was too exhausted to fight it. "You're partly right—I was scared. And I didn't want to go on just living together forever. But I wanted our baby. I meant to raise it myself, if you refused to marry me."

He shoved spread fingers through his hair. "Save it, Kristin. Your father told me the truth."

"My father?" Kristin was confused. Kenyan Meyers hadn't even known about the miscarriage until afterward; he'd been on the other side of the country when it happened.

"He called me about twenty minutes after I came in from that last mission and found you gone." Zachary didn't turn to look at her, and his voice sounded haunted, bewildered; he seemed to be reliving the pain. "He said you had finally come to your senses, that there had been a 'little problem,' but you'd gone to the hospital and had it taken care of."

Kristin was reeling. She'd known all along that her father didn't like Zachary, didn't think he'd make a suitable husband for his only daughter, but she would never have dreamed he was capable of such cruel treachery.

"Damn it," Zachary breathed, whirling around to glare at her in the cold, sparse light, "he called our child a 'little problem'!"

"Zachary—"

He held up one hand to silence her. "No more lies, Kristin. It's better if we just don't talk about this anymore."

Kristin had had enough. She bolted to her feet, using energy from some reserve she hadn't known she possessed, and stormed over to Zachary. "If you think you can drop an emotional bomb like that and then pull your old trick of refusing to talk about it, Zachary Harmon, you're full of sheep dip!''

"Keep your voice down—you'll wake up the whole village!''

"I don't give a damn if I wake up the whole *country*!'' Kristin yelled, hands on her hips, jaw set at an obstinate angle. ''We're going to talk this out! I don't know what he thought gave him the right—and I swear I'm going to strangle him when I get back to Virginia—but my father lied to you. Do you hear me, Zachary? *He lied*. I wanted that baby more than anything else in the world!''

She saw the torment in his eyes, the struggle to believe, and at the same time she knew she'd lost.

It was the final blow; Kristin could bear no more. She turned slowly away from Zachary, lay down on the skins, wrapped herself in one of the blankets and willed herself to die.

"Kristin,'' Zachary said raggedly. And she could feel him reaching for her, with his heart if not his hands. But what did that matter, when he'd take another person's word over hers?

"Leave me alone,'' she whispered, too broken even to cry. She lay curled up throughout the night, caught in that hazy state between waking and sleeping.

In the morning she ate the rice Zachary brought her, but she didn't speak to him. She wasn't punishing him, she wasn't even angry anymore. She simply had nothing to say.

They prepared the bartered plow horses for travel and set out toward the border.

Zachary tried to talk to her again when they stopped for a midday meal of some dried meat Kristin didn't care to categorize. ''We'll be out of Cabriz sometime tomorrow,'' he said.

Kristin just looked at him. She supposed she probably had dark circles under her eyes; she always got them when she was overtired.

"Damn it, will you say something?" Zachary rasped.

She shrugged. "Thank you for saving me from the bad guys," she said. "But then, that's what a macho-man like you is supposed to do, isn't it? Rescue damsels in distress?"

He was plainly annoyed—and he was going to persist in pursuing his point. "Why would your father lie to me?"

"He didn't like you very much," Kristin replied with bald honesty. "I don't suppose it was anything personal—he just thought you had a lousy job. So did I, for that matter. And if I know Dad, he probably ran a background check on you and found something he didn't care for."

Zachary's face tightened, then relaxed again. He threw down the last of his dried meat and hoisted himself upright from a crouching position. "Let's get moving, princess," he said, revealing no emotion at all in his tone. "The evil prince could still catch up with us."

There was no more mention of the lost baby, or of Kristin's father. They traveled in silence, communicating only when necessary. Even when they stopped to make camp they avoided each other as much as possible. At five o'clock the next afternoon they reached the border station Zachary had been aiming for all along.

The Rhaotian guards greeted them with broad grins—the Cabrizians just scowled at Zachary's drawn pistol—and one of the friendly soldiers rushed to telephone the news to their superiors. Soon a representative of the Rhaotian government arrived in a dusty little sedan and, after giving the horses to a surprised farmer as a gift, Zachary and Kristin sped toward Isi, Rhaos's capital city.

Kristin sat numbly in the back seat, her shoulder touching Zachary's, her heart lost in the farthest, loneliest reaches of the universe.

The embassy was in an uproar when they arrived, and reporters waited at the gate, snapping pictures and shouting questions.

Neither Kristin nor Zachary so much as looked in their direction, let alone spoke.

Inside the embassy compound they were immediately separated and subjected to an extensive "debriefing." Kristin told the ambassador and the man from the CIA everything that had happened—except, of course, for the lovemaking. That was private, and she wasn't going to share it with anybody.

"You'd better talk with the reporters, however briefly," the ambassador's assistant advised, after the CIA had subjected Kristin to exhaustive questioning. The aide was a woman in her middle thirties, with sleek dark hair and an air of authority about her. "The whole world has been waiting for a development of some kind."

Kristin's shoulders sagged at the prospect, but before she could frame a reply, the ambassador, an old friend of her father, interceded.

"Great Scott, Caroline, the poor girl is on the verge of collapse. She needs food, rest and perhaps even medical care. Issue some kind of statement to keep them at bay and send for a doctor."

Caroline looked at Kristin reproachfully, but she left the ambassador's study and closed the door behind her.

Mr. Binchly, an old-timer in the diplomatic corps, laid a gentle, beefy hand on Kristin's shoulder. He was a tall man, with a shiny pate and kindly blue eyes. "Were you hurt, Kristin?" he asked, and he looked as though the answer to that question really mattered to him.

A lump formed in Kristin's throat. *Yes,* answered an inner voice, silent but nonetheless eloquent for that. *Yes, I was hurt. I found the man I was meant to love, and he doesn't want me.* "I'll be all right in a few days," she said, and then tears welled up in her eyes.

Mr. Binchly laid his hand lightly on the back of her head and pressed her face to his shoulder. "There, there, you're safe now, dear. We'll see that you get back home to your family as soon as you're ready to travel."

Kristin felt a flicker of rage as she thought of her father, but she suppressed it. She would deal with Kenyan Meyers when she'd recovered her strength. "My friend, Mr. Harmon—is he all right? He was beaten once...." Her voice fell away.

The diplomat seated Kristin in the chair she'd bolted out of after her grueling interview with the CIA and went to pour brandy into a snifter. "Here," he said, handing her the glass. "This will brace you up a little. Harmon is fine, as far as I know. He'll be checked over by a doctor, just as you will."

Kristin nodded distractedly and took a sip of the brandy. The liquor rolled like a fireball down her throat and into her stomach, and her eyes were watering when she looked up. "If I could just lie down—"

"Surely," Mr. Binchly said quickly, and he immediately went to his desk and used his intercom to summon another aide.

Kristin set her brandy aside and followed the young Rhaotian man out of the room with as much dignity as she could manage. He led her up the main staircase and deposited her in a large guest room.

After a brief exploration, Kristin started water running in the bath and asked the aide to send up tea and a platter of fresh fruit. He nodded politely and left.

The bath Kristin took was a leisurely one. She soaked, she washed her hair, she shaved her legs and armpits. And then she let the water out and ran a fresh supply.

When she reentered the bedroom sometime later, wrapped in a towel, she found a white silk robe draped over the back of a chair and a tea tray on the nightstand.

She put on the robe and combed her hair, then sat cross-legged in the middle of the bed with a cup of tea and her journal. Although she'd never been more tired, she felt a need to set down what had happened to her in black and white. Maybe then she'd be able to grapple with the experience and make some sense of it.

Unfortunately, all she could think about was Zachary. Kristin realized now that she'd loved him all along—the episode with Jascha had been a grand-scale attempt to forget her broken heart.

She sighed, cupping her chin in one hand and setting her teacup aside. Zachary was not the kind of man a woman loves once; with him, it was for always. And he couldn't have made it clearer that he wanted nothing whatever to do with her now that they were safe.

Kristin abandoned all attempts to write about her escape from Cabriz and crawled into bed, pulling the covers over her head. She fell into an almost immediate sleep, and didn't awaken until she felt someone pulling back the covers to prod and push at her.

"Zachary," she scolded with a half smile on her face. But when she opened her eyes, she was looking up at a stranger—a doctor, judging by the stethoscope hanging around his neck. He was an Asian of indeterminate age, and his expression was a kindly one.

"I'm sorry not to be Zachary," he said with pleasant formality. "My name is Chong. Paul Chong."

Kristin smiled, despite the sting of disappointment, and sat up, pulling the covers up to her waist. "I really don't need an examination—"

"All the same," interrupted Dr. Chong with a shake of his finger.

"There was a slight injury to my knee," Kristin recalled, frowning. "But a man gave me some sort of tea, and it improved right away."

"Let me see, please," the doctor urged.

Kristin obediently laid the robe aside to reveal her knee. It was still bruised, but there was no swelling and certainly no pain. The doctor examined it with gentle fingers, then covered her.

He nodded thoughtfully. "I wish I had the knowledge of herbs some of the villagers have. They can sometimes accomplish remarkable things."

"Where did you go to school?" Kristin asked cordially as he listened to her chest through his stethoscope.

His smile broadened into a grin. "Harvard," he replied. "If we covered ancient herbal remedies, I must not have been paying attention."

Kristin might have chuckled another time; as it was, she couldn't manage. "Have you seen my friend—Mr. Harmon?"

The doctor took a tongue depressor from his bag, unwrapped it and gestured for Kristin to open her mouth. "He's next on my list."

"Where is he?" Kristin asked, speaking around the wooden stick.

"A few doors down, I think." Dr. Chong tossed the depressor into the wastebasket and took out a little vial of pills. "You are suffering from severe exhaustion, Ms. Meyers. I would like you to take one of these tablets and get some sleep."

"I just want to see Zachary for a minute—"

He handed her one of the pills, along with a glass of water from the carafe on the nightstand. "I will tell him," he said. "In the meantime, please take this."

Kristin threw the pill to the back of her throat and swallowed a gulp of water. "He can be sort of stubborn."

The doctor nodded. "It would require a certain intractability of spirit to effect such a daring escape."

Kristin yawned and sank back against her pillows. "It's not as though he did it all by himself, you know," she pointed out. "He had me to help him."

Chong smiled again. "He is a very fortunate man." With that, he took his bag and left the room.

Eyelids growing heavier with every passing moment, Kristin gazed fixedly at the door. When Zachary came in, she would tell him—well, she didn't know what. There had to be some way to persuade him not to give up on their alliance so easily.

Presently Kristin glanced at the clock on the bedside stand. The doctor had had plenty of time to check Zachary over. So where was that boneheaded ex-spy, anyway?

She tossed back her covers and started to sit up, only to find that the pill and her own fatigue had left her too weak. She sagged back against the pillows and closed her eyes.

Zachary drew up a chair beside the bed and sat down. Taking the note from his shirt pocket, he tucked it into Kristin's journal, which had been lying on the nightstand, and then turned his attention back to her.

Even with her long eyelashes resting on her cheeks, the shadows under Kristin's eyes were evident. Her soft brown hair framed her face, and Zachary could catch the scent of it even from a distance.

He pulled the chair closer, reached out to awaken her, drew back his hand.

God knew, he should have trusted Kristin; he should have been there for her when she was hurting so badly. Instead, just when she'd needed him most, he'd flown into a rage and accused her of something she would never have done.

"Kristin." Her name came out as a raw whisper; she stirred slightly, but didn't open her eyes.

Zachary leaned over and kissed her ever so lightly on the forehead. Her father was a bastard, but he'd probably been right, too. Kristin needed glamour and excitement; she wouldn't be happy in Silver Shores, with a teacher for a husband. She belonged with the jet set.

He couldn't resist touching her mouth with his, and she gave a soft whimper that made his heart turn over.

In the doorway he paused, memorizing her face, her shape, her hair. As if he could ever have forgotten.

"I'm sorry I'm not your prince," he said gruffly. And then he went out.

Kristin awakened feeling physically restored, ate a huge meal, took a shower and dressed in her jeans and T-shirt, which had been laundered for her. "I want to see Mr. Harmon immediately," she told the maid when the woman came in to pick up her tray.

The response was a blank stare and a spate of chatter Kristin didn't understand. All the same, she grasped the fact that the maid didn't speak English and would send someone who did.

The ambassador's wife, Kitty, came in shortly.

"I'm sorry to have bothered you," Kristin told the pretty, middle-aged woman, who had been a college classmate of her mother. "All I really wanted was the precise location of Zachary's room."

Kitty clasped beautifully manicured hands in front of her blue silk sheath, and her brown eyes showed bewilderment. Once, nervously, she touched her fluffy gray hairdo. "You mean Mr. Harmon, of course. Well, Kristin, he's—gone."

Kristin's heart came to a screeching stop, then limped back into its regular beat. "Gone?"

"Oh, I don't mean dead," Kitty said with an endearing smile. "He left yesterday. He said he'd been away from his classes too long."

A hard knot was forming in Kristin's throat. She didn't know Kitty well enough to cry in front of her, so she held on to her dignity with all her strength. "I don't suppose he left a note or anything?"

"Mr. Harmon did ask me to have you look in your journal," she said. "Oh. And you do have a press conference scheduled for this afternoon, if you feel up to it."

Kristin practically dove for the nightstand where she'd left her diary, and flipped it open. Sure enough, there was a folded note tucked between the pages.

"Kris," Zachary had written in his bold, clear hand, "You were right, princess. It will never work. Thanks for all the things we shared. Love, Z."

"Coward," Kristin whispered. And because there were tears in her eyes, she didn't turn to face Kitty. She drew a deep breath and spoke bravely. "I'll take care of the press conference, and then I'd like to leave for the United States as soon after that as possible."

"Caroline will make the arrangements," Kitty promised, and the door closed gently behind her when she went out.

Kristin dried her face with the backs of her hands. Zachary didn't want her and, since that was something she couldn't change, she would have to accept it.

She used the makeup either Kitty or Caroline had so kindly lent her, and then she took her journal, went out into the courtyard and wrote until her fingers were too numb to hold the pen. After that she marched stoically into the embassy, met with eager representatives of the press from all over the world and told them her story.

Except for the parts she regarded as personal, Kristin told the complete, unvarnished truth. And she didn't cry once, the whole time.

"Your rescuer was Zachary Harmon," called out one American reporter, an attractive woman smiling thoughtfully. "Weren't you and he romantically involved at one time?"

Kristin swallowed, but her gaze snapped with anger. "I hardly see what that has to do with anything," she said curtly.

The reporter was undaunted. In fact, her smile widened. "Well, it might make this into quite a different story. Didn't you and Mr. Harmon live together once?"

There was a general buzz among the others while Kristin frantically formulated an answer.

"Zachary—Mr. Harmon and I were involved some time ago," she said, keeping her tones even. "But that's all over now. There's nothing between us."

With that, Kristin pushed back her chair and stood. Flashbulbs went off all over the room, blinding her, and she went out gripping Ambassador Binchly's arm.

Early the next morning she boarded an airplane. It touched down in Singapore, then Honolulu. Kristin would have a four-hour layover there before flying on to the mainland.

Since her passport was still in Cabriz, Kristin had special papers from the ambassador to show at customs.

Her mother was there when she finished, however, and the surprise was a welcome one. Kristin flung herself into Alice Meyers's arms with abandon.

Alice embraced her daughter, one gracious hand pressing the back of Kristin's head. "Dear heaven," she said with tears in her voice. "We thought we'd lost you."

Kristin stiffened. "You haven't," she said, putting only the slightest emphasis on the word *you*. She would discuss her father's part in her initial breakup with Zachary when they reached Virginia.

Crystal-blue eyes swept over Kristin's clothes. "Just as I thought. You need to do some shopping before we go home." Alice linked her arm with Kristin's, and they started toward the door. There was no point in going to baggage claim, since Kristin had nothing but the clothes she was wearing and her journal. "I have a lovely room at the Hilton. We could swim and sunbathe and shop and talk—"

"Not all at once, I hope," Kristin said with a faltering smile. It was the closest thing to a joke she'd be able to manage for a long time, she suspected.

"It was Zachary who came and got you, wasn't it?" Alice pressed when they were settled in the back of a cab and heading toward the hotel.

Kristin nodded, biting her lower lip.

Alice reached out, took her daughter's hand and squeezed it. "I don't imagine Jascha was happy to see you leave," she said, probably sensing that the subject of Zachary was painful for Kristin.

She shook her head and said nothing, hoping her mother would guess that she didn't want to talk about Jascha, either. Not just yet.

"Well, you'll be almost as good as new by the time you've had a few days in the sunshine and restocked your wardrobe," Alice stated, still valiantly searching for a safe topic. "I think we ought to spend a great deal of your father's money."

Kristin nodded, watching the familiar beach and dazzling blue ocean slip past the cab window. "How's the weather back in Virginia?" she asked, mostly to rescue Alice.

The older woman shivered. "Chilly. After all, dear, it's nearly Thanksgiving. It won't be long until we have snow. Perhaps if your father can get away we'll all fly down to Bermuda and have our turkey dinner there."

"No," Kristin said. "I mean, I just want to have a few words with Dad, then I'll be going back to L.A. Or maybe to New York."

Wisely, Alice didn't push. She was no slouch when it came to diplomacy herself, having spent all those years in Cabriz.

When they reached the hotel, Kristin bought a swimsuit in one of the shops. After putting the garment on in the suite Alice had rented, she went out to the pool and swam rapid laps, moving with such determination that the other tourists got out of her way.

Only when her arms refused to make another stroke did she grasp the tiled side of the pool and whisk the hair back from her face.

Alice was sitting comfortably in a lounge chair, sipping a colorful tropical drink. Her stylish dark hair was neatly covered by a white bathing cap. "I'm exhausted just from watching you, dear," she said, taking a maraschino cherry from her cocktail and popping it into her mouth.

Kristin was studying her mother, seeing signs of strain around her eyes and mouth. Although no one else was nearby, she lowered her voice. "You were frightened for me, weren't you, Mother?" she asked gently.

"Yes," Alice answered. "Fortunately, we didn't know what had really gone on until after you reached the embassy in Rhaos. Mr. Binchly called your father right away, of course, and told him the whole story.''

Not the whole story, Kristin thought sadly, remembering how Zachary had held her, caressed her, made her cry out in the night because the pleasure was too keen to be endured in silence. "I'm sorry you were worried. I should have known better than to think a marriage between Jascha and I could work, especially when the Cabrizian government was toppling.''

Alice set her drink on a table, approached the pool and lowered herself into the water beside Kristin. "Jascha seemed like such a charming young man when you used to bring him home from school," she said fretfully. "What happened?''

Kristin shrugged. "He was putting on a facade for all of us back in the States, I think," she speculated. "But in Cabriz, he was surrounded by his own culture. And that required that he have more than one wife, among other things.''

A sigh escaped Alice. "Don't think your father and I don't blame ourselves for what's happened. We lived in Cabriz for years. We *knew* the culture permitted a man of Jascha's status to marry more than once. It's just that he seemed so westernized, and he promised us he loved only you.''

Gently, Kristin laid a hand on her mother's shoulder. "It wasn't your fault. I was chasing fairy tales long after I should have grown up.''

Alice reached out, smoothed a tendril of wet hair away from Kristin's cheek. "That hollow look I see in your eyes— it's there because of Zachary, isn't it? Kristin, what really happened in Cabriz?''

Kristin swallowed and averted her eyes for a moment. She wasn't sure she could keep the truth from her mother, wasn't sure she even wanted to. "I think I was on the verge of getting Zachary back. But I lost him, Mother. I lost him all over again, and it's tearing me apart."

"This calls for a drink," Alice replied, and held up one hand to call over a waiter.

Kristin asked for white wine and stood at the side of the pool sipping it as she told her mother how deeply she'd cared for Zachary.

"What are you going to do now?" Alice asked when her daughter had finished.

Kristin sighed, studying the blue Hawaiian sky. "I want to have a few words with Dad—in person—and then I'm going to hole up in an apartment somewhere—pick a city, any city—and write. Zachary aside, I have one hell of a story to tell."

She and Alice left the pool behind after that, along with the subject of Kristin's adventure. They spent the coming days just as they'd planned to—shopping, sunning, relaxing.

When Kristin flew on to the mainland, she was tanned, rested and ready to do battle, first with her father, then with the world.

On her first night back, network newscasters announced to the world that the Cabrizian government had fallen. Jascha had escaped with his life and was living in exile in Singapore.

Eleven

Kristin's father rose from behind his desk and came toward her, arms extended for a hug. She drew back against the towering study doors, her manner wary, and his delighted expression faded.

"What is it?" he asked.

"Sit down—please," she said woodenly.

When Kenyan had returned, albeit reluctantly, to his leather swivel chair, his daughter took a seat facing his desk.

"A year and a half ago, when I miscarried, you called Zachary and told him I'd had an abortion instead. I'd like to know why."

Kenyan's gray hair glinted in the light of his desk lamp, and his face was in shadows. "I think you know, Kristin," he said reasonably. "Harmon was a government agent. The things he's done, independently and by order of his superiors, would horrify you. And his background couldn't have been more dissimilar to yours—''

Kristin's hands tightened on the arms of her chair and, for virtually the first time in her life, she interrupted her father. "My God, Dad, I *loved* the man—I was living with him, expecting his baby. How could you interfere like that? What gave you the right?''

His voice rose slightly as he replied, "You had already left Harmon, remember? I merely wanted your decision to stand. And the fact that you're my daughter gave me the right, damn it!''

The reminder that she had been the one to instigate the whole problem in the first place brought pulsing color to Kristin's cheeks. "I was wrong, Dad," she said brokenly. "I should have stayed and tried to work things out with Zachary. But that doesn't change the fact that you had no business messing with my life.''

Kenyan sighed heavily. "Harmon would never make a good husband or father," he said. "The man has no conception of what family life means.''

"And you do, I suppose?" Kristin demanded, leaning forward in her chair. "Are lying and meddling things a father should do?''

The ambassador-turned-cabinet-member held up one hand in a bid for silence. "I'm willing to concede that what I did was wrong, Kristin. But I still maintain that Harmon wouldn't be able to give you what you need.''

Kristin's tone was cordially acid. "Which is?''

"A regular home.''

"Come on, Dad. What did you find out about Zachary that worried you so much? That he cheated on a third-grade history test? That he was raised by his grandfather?''

"Damn it," Kenyan blurted, slamming one fist down on the desktop, "both his parents were alcoholics. There was an automobile accident and not only were the Harmons killed outright, so were a young mother and her two children, on their way home from the supermarket!"

Sickness rushed into Kristin's throat as she thought of what Zachary and his grandfather must have suffered, along with the family of the mother and children. "That wasn't Zachary's fault," she said softly.

"I'm not saying it was," Kenyan insisted, his face flushed with conviction and, probably, the desire to redeem himself. "But things like that tend to run in families. Forgive me, Kristin, but I didn't want it running in ours!"

At last she stood. "That wasn't your decision to make," she said calmly. "Now, if you'll excuse me, I've got some packing to do."

Outside, a light snow was drifting down from gray afternoon skies. The view framed Kenyan's impressive physique as he stood to protest. "You're leaving? But it's almost Thanksgiving. Your mother—"

Kristin paused at the doors and turned to face him again. "I suppose I'll forgive you, in time. After all, I love you very much, God help me. But right now I don't want to be in the same state with you, Dad, let alone the same house. Goodbye."

"Kristin, I've apologized!"

She hesitated, her hand on the doorknob. "To me, yes," she conceded. "But not to Zachary." With that, she walked out of the study and climbed the stairs. In her room, she cried as she packed.

Five hours later she landed in New York, a destination chosen for its proximity to the publishing world, checked into a hotel room and set up her computer. Writing about her experiences in Cabriz would be her salvation; it would give her life focus and meaning.

She hoped.

Kristin worked straight through Thanksgiving, making no telephone calls and marking the occasion only with a turkey sandwich from the coffee shop down the street. Although she didn't allow herself to think about him consciously, Zachary hovered at the edges of her life like a phantom.

The week before Christmas, Kristin was finally ready to show her work to someone. She'd drafted an extensive outline of her prospective book, and had written the first chapter.

She called John Claridge, a family friend in the publishing business, and he eagerly agreed to look at her proposal. Of course, that left her with a holiday to face and nothing to keep her occupied until it had passed. Since she was in New York, Christmas was everywhere; the only way to avoid it would be to hide out in her hotel room. And Kristin couldn't do that, not without the book to absorb her attention.

She finally telephoned her mother.

Alice wept with relief. "Kristin! Are you all right? In the name of heaven, where are you?"

"New York," Kristin answered, and gave her mother the name of the hotel. "Listen, I was just thinking, well, maybe I could come home for Christmas?"

"Of course you can," Alice was quick to sniffle. "What time will your plane be in?"

"I'll take a train tomorrow, Mother," Kristin answered a moment after the idea came to her. "I want some time to think about a few things."

"You've had phone calls," Alice told her in the same tone of voice she'd used years before, when Kristin had been full of Christmas curiosity and there were presents hidden all over the house.

Kristin's heart leaped out of its normal beat and hammered at the base of her throat. "From whom?"

Alice hesitated. "Zachary Harmon, for one. He left several numbers. Would you like them?"

"No," Kristin said impulsively. "Who else called?"

As if you cared, her mother's tone of voice replied. "Just some of your college friends, dear. I'll tell you all about it when you get home."

Zachary's name buzzed in Kristin's heart like a pesky bee hovering around a picnic while she packed her clothes and arranged for her computer to be shipped back to Virginia. She had no idea where she'd be going after that.

All during the train ride the following day she thought about the man who had rescued her from Cabriz. The fact that his parents had been alcoholics explained Zachary's difficulty with trust and his fear of commitment. It must have been hell, growing up knowing the two people who had given him life were responsible for taking that same gift from others.

"Oh, Zachary," she whispered, staring out the window at the wintry countryside. "If I had it all to do over again, I'd change so many things."

When the train pulled into the station at Williamsburg, Alice Meyers was there to meet Kristin, looking splendid in a full-length mink coat and matching hat. She embraced her daughter and took her arm, leading her straightaway to the waiting car. The baggage would be sent out later.

"I haven't done any shopping," Kristin mused, seeing that lights and decorations were everywhere. It was a giant commercial conspiracy, and yet she loved Christmas.

Alice squeezed her arm. "We still have tomorrow," she said. "Tell me, what have you been doing?"

"Working on a book," Kristin confessed. "I gave the outline and the first chapter to John Claridge to read. Now there's nothing to do but wait."

Alice had a mysterious look on her face. "I think there's much more to do than that, dear," she answered sweetly. Then she opened the car door and got behind the wheel.

"What are you trying to tell me?" Kristin asked, a smile tugging at the corners of her mouth.

Her mother simply shrugged. "Nothing at all."

Kristin fastened her seat belt as Alice started the car. "You said Zachary called," she ventured. "What did he say?"

The engine roared, and the large car rolled into traffic. Alice shrugged one mink-swathed shoulder. "He asked for your number. Of course, I couldn't give it to him since I didn't know what it was myself."

Kristin sighed. "It's just as well," she said, putting down the springing hope she'd felt at the news.

Alice said nothing more about Zachary. She simply drove through the familiar streets of Williamsburg and came to a stop in front of the Meyers's house. There was a funny-looking compact car blocking the driveway, and the lights were burning in Kenyan's study.

Kristin glanced in her mother's direction, but Alice was studiously avoiding her gaze. The two women entered the house by way of a door with an enormous holly wreath hung upon it.

"We're here!" Alice cried gleefully, shrugging out of her coat and shaking off the snowflakes. That done, she hung the garment and hat neatly in the closet, and not once did she glance in her daughter's direction.

The study doors opened, and Kristin froze where she was. Standing there in the chasm, looking as uncomfortable as she felt, stood Zachary Harmon. He loosened his tie and swallowed visibly as he ran his eyes over her.

"Hello, Kristin," he finally said, and his voice was hoarse.

Kristin's muscles became mobile again, and she unbuttoned her coat and hung it in the closet with her mother's. "What are you doing here?"

He rested his hands on his hips. "Well, that's one hell of a greeting," he grumbled as Alice crept past him into the study and closed the doors. "I came to get you—that's what I'm doing here."

A tangle of sensations gushed up inside Kristin like a geyser. "You thought I'd just let you take me by the hair and drag me back to your cave, huh?"

Zachary loomed above her now, and his hazel eyes snapped with annoyance. "Why don't you just keep quiet and listen for once?" he barked. "I'm here because I love you, damn it. Because my life isn't worth a pile of wet seaweed without you. And the least you could do is listen while I tell you I'm sorry I didn't trust you before!"

Kristin stared at him, wide-eyed. "Dad admitted he lied?"

"He didn't have to. I knew." Zachary came to her, bundled her into her coat and put on his own. "Come on. We're going somewhere where we can talk." With that, he shuffled her out of the house, down the driveway and into the ugly little car.

"I hope you rented this," Kristin said. She was in such a state of shock that inanities were all she could manage.

Zachary tossed her a wan grin. "That's your first wish, princess. You have two more coming." He pulled into the sluggish, early-evening traffic typical of the neighborhood.

Barely able to believe he was really there, Kristin reached out and touched his upper arm. It felt sturdy and solid beneath her fingers and the cloth of his coat. "I love you, Zachary," she said.

He laughed, and there was something merry in the sound, a release of old ideas and fears. "Hey," he protested, "that's *my* wish."

"Well, I'm granting it," Kristin replied softly, letting her head rest against his shoulder. "I don't know if we can make a go of it now any more than we did then, but there's no question that I'm in love with you. Hopelessly."

Zachary's lips touched the top of her head. "We'll start with that, then, and work out the rest as we go along. Tell me what you've been doing."

Kristin looked up into his face. "I've been missing you, mostly. Though I did manage to work up a proposal for a book about Cabriz."

He grinned. "I suppose you left out the fact that I can drive you crazy in bed," he said.

She laughed and jabbed him lightly in the ribs. "I did leave that out, in fact," she replied. "But since you also drive me crazy everywhere else, there was no lack of material."

Zachary guided the car through the snowy streets, coming to a stop in front of a coffee shop across the street from an historic inn with a boastful sign on the lawn. "That George Washington sure got around," he muttered as he helped Kristin from the car.

They entered the coffee shop, which was almost deserted, and took a table at the rear. Once the waitress had brought them both steaming cups of espresso and left them alone again, Zachary reached across the table and took both Kristin's hands in his.

"That's terrific—that you started a book, I mean," he said gravely.

Kristin shrugged. "I haven't sold it, Zachary. And there's a big difference between starting and selling."

"It'll be a hit," he said with quiet certainty. "You're a good writer, Kris."

She felt defensive. After all, Zachary had never said a positive word about her efforts, either before their breakup or after they'd gotten together in Cabriz. "How do you know?"

"I've been following your career for the last year and a half, that's how. Maybe the subject matter left something wanting but—"

Kristin's cheeks reddened. "Okay, so I wrote about parties," she snapped. "The editors wouldn't trust me with anything but fluff!"

"Calm down," Zachary said. "I'm not criticizing you. I really believe this book is your chance to make a name for yourself."

She found herself itching to show him a copy of the work she'd done so far. "What were you and Dad talking about when I came in?"

He sighed and sat back in the booth. "You, of course. He apologized—albeit grudgingly—for lying to me, and I asked him for your hand in marriage."

Kristin's cup stopped midway between the saucer and her lips. "You did what?"

"You're an old-fashioned girl, Kris, or you wouldn't have been sucked into that whole fairy-tale setup over in Cabriz. So I flew out here—after your mother called and told me you were coming—and asked your father if I could marry you. Of course, if he'd said no, I still would have proposed to you."

"He said yes?"

Zachary nodded, a grin lifting one corner of his mouth. "What about you, Kris? Are you going to say yes, too?"

She hesitated, but not because there was any question in her mind. She was just wondering if this was really happening. "If I do, where will we live?"

"I like Silver Shores," Zachary replied. "I have a cozy little beach house there. But if that doesn't work for you, then we'll find something else. Now, would you mind putting me out of my misery and answering my question?"

"Yes."

"Yes, you'll answer my question, or yes, you'll marry me?"

"Yes, I'll marry you. Gladly. But we've got to promise each other one thing—there'll be no refusing to talk about things—"

"And no running away from a problem," Zachary interceded, leaning forward and raising his eyebrows.

Kristin nodded. "I regret leaving you, Zachary," she said. "With all my heart."

He got out his wallet and laid a bill on the table to pay the check and cover the tip. "Let's get out of here."

"Where are we going?" Kristin asked. He hadn't even kissed her, and her heart was fluttering like a trapped bird. Her body seemed to be opening up to Zachary, preparing for him, and the heat that surged through her was surely glowing in her face.

"We're going to buy a ring," he answered. "And a license."

"No storybook wedding?"

He faced her, his fingers locking gently over her shoulders. "Is that what you want, princess? A white dress and all the trimmings? If it is, we'll wait."

Kristin swallowed. "The last thing I want to do is wait, Zachary. If you don't make love to me, I'm going to burst."

He caught his forefinger under her chin, lifted, and gave her a teasing kiss on the mouth. "Don't worry, babe. I'm going to love you all night long. But first I want an engagement ring on your finger, at the very least. And some promises have to be made."

Kristin looked up at him. "What are we going to tell my parents if we stay out all night?"

Zachary was helping her into her coat again. "I don't suppose we'll have to tell them anything. They're intelligent people—" he paused to nibble at the side of her neck "—they'll figure out what's going on."

An hour later the two of them selected a beautiful diamond ring in a nearby jewelry store, and Zachary slipped it on her finger right there in front of the clerk. Then he pulled Kristin close and kissed her thoroughly, while the onlookers applauded.

By the time they were back in Zachary's car, Kristin was in a heightened state of anticipation. She looked hopefully at every decent hotel and inn they passed, but Zachary didn't stop. He drove straight to her parents' house.

"I want to tell them we're getting married," he explained.

"But just a little while ago, you said they'd figure it out for themselves—"

"They would. After going through hell picturing you dead beside the highway because of some accident."

Kristin nodded and got out of the car, and she and Zachary linked arms as they walked toward the house. Kenyan and Alice were waiting for them in the entryway.

"Zachary and I are getting married as soon as possible," Kristin said.

Alice looked disappointed. "But I've always dreamed of giving you a beautiful wedding—"

"Great Scott, Alice," Kenyan interrupted, "can't you see they're hardly able to wait as it is? The kind of shindig you're thinking of takes months to prepare."

Kristin went to her mother, took both her hands. "We could still have a formal wedding, if it means so much to you. But there has to be a ceremony *soon*."

Kenyan's eyes widened, and he looked at Zachary with renewed rage. "By God, Harmon—"

"I'm not pregnant, Dad," Kristin said. Then she glanced back at Zachary. "Not yet, anyway."

"Just how soon would you two like to be married?" Kenyan asked.

"Tonight," Zachary answered without a moment's hesitation.

"I suppose that could be arranged," Kenyan said, his expression thoughtful. He had lots of friends in high places, naturally, and a simple marriage license would not be hard to expedite. His gaze turned to Kristin. "You're sure?"

She nodded.

"Very well, then," Kenyan responded, extending a hand to Zachary. "I hope you and I can let bygones be bygones, Harmon. I love Kristin, and I want her to be happy."

Zachary shook his future father-in-law's hand. "There's something we agree on," he said quietly.

The ceremony was performed an hour later, in Kenyan's study, by a very distinguished judge who had also arranged for a special license. There were flowers from the greenhouse, and Kristin wore the same lacy, romantic dress she'd worn when she'd danced with Zachary at that long-ago Christmas party.

The slight flush on his face and the sparkle in his eyes told Kristin he remembered not only the dress but the episode on the pool table as well.

Kenyan took pictures with his personal camera, and Alice severed fruitcake in lieu of wedding cake. When the Meyerses were satisfied that the occasion had been duly celebrated, Alice said with a sniffle, "I've had the guest house prepared as a honeymoon cottage. If you need anything, just use the intercom and someone will see that you get it."

Zachary loosened his tie again, and Kristin felt his fingers tighten around hers. "Great," he said.

A few minutes later he carried her, laughing, down the snowy, slippery walk to the guest house and over the threshold. Inside the one-bedroom cottage, there was a fire blazing on the fieldstone hearth, and a bottle of Kenyan's best champagne was cooling on ice.

Zachary gave a teasing growl, then covered Kristin's mouth with his own, still holding her in his arms. She whimpered as a fire kindled deep within her and then grew hotter with every passing moment. Her arms tightened around Zachary's neck, and her tongue sparred with his.

Finally, with a gasp, he tore his lips from hers, carried Kristin into the bedroom and dropped her unceremoniously on the bed.

Kristin's heart beat faster as she watched her husband undo his tie and toss it aside, then shrug out of his suit coat.

A tremor went through her. "Is this the part where you love me all night long?"

"This is the part," he replied, beginning to unbutton his shirt. "I hope you're in top shape, princess, because you're about to get a workout."

Kristin kicked off her shoes, but that was all the undressing Zachary would allow her to do. He took off her stockings personally, kissing each of her knees as he bared them, then tossed aside her voluminous petticoats. After that, he lifted her to her feet long enough to divest her of the dress, and she was naked before him.

She reached for the fastener on his slacks, but he caught hold of her hand and lifted it to his mouth, kissing the palm lightly, then flicking it with his tongue.

Kristin drew in a harsh breath, and her eyes drifted closed. "Zachary..."

He lifted her, just as he'd had to carry her to the guest house, and raised her high enough that he could take one of her nipples into his mouth.

Kristin cried out and arched her back, making herself more available. Zachary took her to the rug in front of the fireplace, enjoying her all the while, and laid her gently on the floor.

She stretched as she watched him open his trousers and remove them, held out her arms when he lowered himself to her side. The light of the fire danced over their bodies like some sort of pagan blessing.

"I love you," Zachary whispered, his lips tasting the length of Kristin's neck even as his hand deftly separated her legs.

She gasped with pleasure when she felt one of his fingers burrow in to prepare her. "And I love you—oh—so much—oh, Zachary..."

He chuckled, nuzzled her breasts, boldly captured a nipple. "Umm?" he asked, suckling at the same time.

Kristin writhed as he clasped her moist mound in his hand and slipped deft fingers inside her. The heel of his palm moved against the sweetest secret of her womanhood. "Love me—oh, please—love me *now*! You have all night to tease!"

Zachary nudged her legs apart with one knee and cradled himself between them, his fingers still working their singular magic. He bent his head and touched one of her nipples with his tongue, training it to pebble hardness. "You shock me, Mrs. Harmon. Are you asking me to consummate this marriage?"

"Yes, damn you!" Kristin cried, her eyes closed, her head back, her hips rising and falling under Zachary's hand. "Yes!"

He withdrew his fingers and clasped his hands under Kristin's bottom. She felt his shaft pressing against her, gave a long, crooning moan as it slid inside her.

She tried to raise herself, to start the friction she needed so badly, but Zachary stilled her by grasping her hips. "Easy," he breathed, giving her another slow, delicious stroke.

Kristin cried out, her fingers flying over Zachary's back, searching for a handhold, a way to push him into her. He teased until she flung her legs around him and imprisoned him in her depths, then his control snapped.

He grated out her name and bent to suckle briefly, desperately, at each of her breasts. Then, raising himself onto his hands, he drove into her powerfully, withdrew, and drove again.

Kristin lowered her legs, heels digging into the rug as she hurled herself at Zachary, receiving every lunge, welcoming it. Her head tossed from side to side and her hair was a wild tangle around her face, but she didn't care.

She matched Zachary stroke for stroke, and when her body began to convulse, gripping his, drawing at it, she pulled his head down and took his mouth with her own. He stayed with the kiss as long as he could, but then his powerful body buckled and he flung back his head. A low, muffled shout came from his throat as he gave himself up in final surrender.

When it was over, Kristin held him close, running her hands over his back to soothe him. She was too exhausted to talk, and there were tears glimmering in her eyes—tears she didn't want him to see.

He rolled onto his back, pulling Kristin with him, holding her close. A long time passed before either of them spoke.

"I want you to quit the birth control as soon as possible," Zachary said.

Kristin laughed. "Mother's doctor already took care of that, handsome. You and I had broken up, and I didn't plan on sleeping with anybody else."

"Good. Then let's get down to some serious baby making." He rolled onto his side, smiling, and traced the circumference of her nipples with his fingertip. Kristin felt sweet tension coiling inside her, knowing it would only be a matter of minutes before he suckled her. "I'd like to be a father by this time next year."

Kristin pulled a face. "Oh, yeah? How do you plan to manage that?"

"By taking you to bed on a very regular basis." The words rumbled from his throat; he was already kissing the plump breast he'd selected. "I'll come home for—" he paused to draw her into his mouth and enjoy her for a few moments "—lunch. And, of course, when I get back from school in the afternoon, you'll be through writing and ready to welcome me properly."

Kristin could no longer bear to lie still; she began to stroke him gently in retaliation. "Of course," she purred.

"Oh, Kris—"

"And there will be times, naturally, when I'll visit you during the day. Your office door does have a lock, doesn't it?" She nipped at his earlobe with her teeth, was delighted by Zachary's lively response. "Doesn't it?" she repeated.

"Yes," Zachary groaned, completely in her power.

Kristin felt both triumph and passion as she maneuvered her husband into position for another session of loving. This time, she wouldn't have to plead.

He would.

And she was prepared to be generous.

*   *   *   *   *

Take 4 bestselling love stories FREE

Plus get a FREE surprise gift!

PASSPORT TO ROMANCE
SWEEPSTAKES RULES

1. **HOW TO ENTER:** To enter, you must be the age of majority and complete the official entry form, or print your name, address, telephone number and age on a plain piece of paper and mail to: Passport to Romance, P.O. Box 9056, Buffalo, NY 14269-9056. No mechanically reproduced entries accepted.

2. All entries must be received by the CONTEST CLOSING DATE, DECEMBER 31, 1990 TO BE ELIGIBLE.

3. **THE PRIZES:** There will be ten (10) Grand Prizes awarded, each consisting of a choice of a trip for two people from the following list:
   i) London, England (approximate retail value $5,050 U.S.)
   ii) England, Wales and Scotland (approximate retail value $6,400 U.S.)
   iii) Carribean Cruise (approximate retail value $7,300 U.S.)
   iv) Hawaii (approximate retail value $9,550 U.S.)
   v) Greek Island Cruise in the Mediterranean (approximate retail value $12,250 U.S.)
   vi) France (approximate retail value $7,300 U.S.)

4. Any winner may choose to receive any trip or a cash alternative prize of $5,000.00 U.S. in lieu of the trip.

5. **GENERAL RULES:** Odds of winning depend on number of entries received.

6. A random draw will be made by Nielsen Promotion Services, an independent judging organization, on January 29, 1991, in Buffalo, NY, at 11.30 a.m. from all eligible entries received on or before the Contest Closing Date.

7. Any Canadian entrants who are selected must correctly answer a time-limited, mathematical skill-testing question in order to win.

8. Full contest rules may be obtained by sending a stamped, self-addressed envelope to: "Passport to Romance Rules Request" P.O. Box 9998, Saint John, New Brunswick, Canada E2L 4N4.

9. Quebec residents may submit any litigation respecting the conduct and awarding of a prize in this contest to the Régie des loteries et courses du Québec.

10. Payment of taxes other than air and hotel taxes is the sole responsibility of the winner.

11. Void where prohibited by law.

COUPON BOOKLET OFFER TERMS

To receive your Free travel-savings coupon booklets, complete the mail-in Offer Certificate on the preceeding page, including the necessary number of proofs-of-purchase, and mail to: Passport to Romance, P.O. Box 9057, Buffalo, NY 14269-9057 The coupon booklets include savings on travel-related products such as car rentals, hotels, cruises, flowers and restaurants. Some restrictions apply The offer is available in the United States and Canada. Requests must be postmarked by January 25, 1991 Only proofs-of-purchase from specially marked "Passport to Romance" Harlequin® or Silhouette® books will be accepted. The offer certificate must accompany your request and may not be reproduced in any manner. Offer void where prohibited or restricted by law LIMIT FOUR COUPON BOOKLETS PER NAME, FAMILY, GROUP, ORGANIZATION OR ADDRESS. Please allow up to 8 weeks after receipt of order for shipment Enter quickly as quantities are limited. Unfulfilled mail-in offer requests will receive free Harlequin® or Silhouette® books (not previously available in retail stores), in quantities equal to the number of proofs-of-purchase required for Levels One to Four, as applicable.

OFFICIAL SWEEPSTAKES
ENTRY FORM

Complete and return this Entry Form immediately—the more Entry Forms you submit, the better your chances of winning!
- Entry Forms must be received by **December 31, 1990**
- A random draw will take place on **January 29, 1991**   3-SD-1-SW
- Trip must be taken by **December 31, 1991**

YES, I want to win a PASSPORT TO ROMANCE vacation for two! I understand the prize includes round-trip air fare, accommodation and a daily spending allowance.

Name_____

Address_____

City_____ State_____ Zip_____

Telephone Number_____ Age_____

Return entries to: **PASSPORT TO ROMANCE**, P.O. Box 9056, Buffalo, NY 14269-9056

COUPON BOOKLET/OFFER CERTIFICATE

Item	LEVEL ONE Booklet 1	LEVEL TWO Booklet 1 & 2	LEVEL THREE Booklet 1, 2 & 3	LEVEL FOUR Booklet 1, 2, 3 & 4
Booklet 1 = $100+	$100+	$100+	$100+	$100+
Booklet 2 = $200+		$200+	$200+	$200+
Booklet 3 = $300+			$300+	$300+
Booklet 4 = $400+	____	____	____	$400+
Approximate Total Value of Savings	$100+	$300+	$600+	$1,000+
# of Proofs of Purchase Required	4	6	12	18
Check One	____	____	____	____

Name_____

Address_____

City_____ State_____ Zip_____

Return Offer Certificates to: **PASSPORT TO ROMANCE**, P.O. Box 9057, Buffalo, NY 14269-9057

Requests must be postmarked by **January 25, 1991**

ONE PROOF OF PURCHASE   3-SD-1

To collect your free coupon booklet you must include the necessary number of proofs-of-purchase with a properly completed Offer Certificate

See previous page for details